SHIBBOLETH

SHIBBOLETH

JAMES D. SULLIVAN

Copyright © James D. Sullivan 2015

ISBN: 978-1-943170-07-4

Cover Design: Jane L. Carman

Interior Design: Paige Domantey

Production Director: Jane L. Carman

Typefaces: Garamond and Imperator Bronze

Published by: Lit Fest Press, Carman, 688 Knox Road 900 North, Gilson, Illinois 61436

There are no rules.
festivalwriter.org

CONTENTS

SAMSON
JUDGES 14-16

1.

Philistine women really turned him on, but their uncircumcised men disgusted him. Their unwashed foreskins must fill up with filth. Just imagine those dirty shafts inside their vaginas—how much they must want a clean, strong Israelite cockhead. He liked Philistine prostitutes. He could see in the bitter almonds of their eyes as he approached, feel beneath their tensing skin as he touched them how they must be comparing his wholesome and powerful physique with the puny, corrupted flesh of their countrymen. He imagined them all longing for him. And these women, unlike his Israelite sisters, would never bear the honorable destiny of God's chosen nation, so they didn't matter. They fell outside of sacred history, so he could take them in his butcher's hands and do what he liked. Among Philistine women, he could be uninhibitedly dirty and then rise from their louse-ridden cots still the clean-souled hero of Israel, righteous scourge of idolatrous, uncircumcised nations who dared block God's sacred plan.

Samson himself was rigorously clean. His never-cut hair glistened. His body had never tasted wine nor grape. His hand wouldn't even recognize the texture of a vinestock. A Nazarite from conception, raised by his parents to clean this holy land of the filthy nations the Israelite tribes had found living there, Samson knew all along that his destiny was to kill Philistines. But he loved Philistine women.

In the marketplace of the Philistine town of Timnath, he happened to see a young woman with beauty like an elegantly gloved fist, achingly delicate, yet she weakened him like a sock in the breastbone. He had to have her just to recover his equilibrium. So he made some inquiries. A decent girl from a good family, she was not available for a bit of cash. Damn. He had to marry her.

Well, so be it. So he went home to Dan and asked his father to make suitable arrangements with her family for a wedding. Accustomed to getting what he wanted from parents who had raised him to think of himself as a Man of Destiny, he simply told them, "I've seen this woman in Timnath, daughter of some Philistines. Get her for me to marry."

"'Get her for me.' That's all you have to say? You know you're speaking to your father? Who is this girl?" Naturally, they were interested in seeing their son marry. But a Philistine? "You're telling me there's no likely girl here among the neighbors? No nice Israelite girls, so you have to go find yourself a wife among those filthy, uncircumcised Philistines? What is this craziness?"

"Get her for me. Trust me: she looks all right. I want her."

But marrying an idolatrous foreigner was hardly part of the destiny Manoah and his wife had imagined for their son. They knew about his dalliances with foreign prostitutes—actions that hardly befit a Nazarite, of course, but wild oats and all that, boys will be etc. He'd grow out of that and settle down. No, not settle down. They actually expected him to become a great leader, another Joshua, cleaning the land of the nation's enemies, clearing room for the ever-multiplying eminence of Israel's posterity. They saw their son, like Joshua (like Montezuma) offer the blood of whole nations as a sacrifice toward their One God. The boy had always been gratifyingly contemptuous of foreigners. You might even say whoring Philistine girls was another way to show his contempt for them, no? But now? Should a Nazarite marry an idol worshiper?

Anybody could become, like Samson, a Nazarite, dedicating some specific, limited period of life to God. As outward signs of this period of sanctity, the Nazarite was to avoid all wine, grapes, grape leaves, or any other product of the vine, and till the end of the time dedicated, never get a haircut. Samson's mother, to ensure her child's total sanctity throughout his entire imaginable existence, had herself taken the Nazarite vow before she conceived him and continued it throughout her pregnancy and till she weaned him. So he never, even indirectly, ingested any grape or grape products, and of course, his parents never cut his hair. Though certainly the option of lifelong Nazarite status lay within the law, people just didn't do that. Since there was, however, no actual rule about the length of Nazarite dedication, why not a whole life? On their son's behalf, Manoah and his wife just took this pious practice to a unique extreme. They raised him to believe in his own special holiness and that he held God's own power in his arms. They raised him to hate Philistines.

So with his parents, Samson travelled down to Timnath to arrange marriage with one. (Yes, they gave in. They always did.) At one point along the journey, he wandered off while his parents set camp by a brook. He happened upon a lion cub, who offered a feeble little baby roar at this man blundering into his territory. The big kitten tried to scare him. Samson thought that was hilarious, so he bent over to pick it up. It scratched him. Instinctively replying blow for blow, he grabbed it by the throat, plunged a hand up under the rib cage, and tore. He washed his hands in the brook, then ambled back upstream toward his parents. He felt good; killing the lion relieved much of the sexual and social anxiety building up in him as he approached the marriage bargain. He would not ruin the sensation by telling his parents about the lion and provoking their tiresome, pointless, hind-sight worries.

They struck a deal with the young woman's family, all in a spirit of cooperation between these two peoples sharing this fruitful land. Here's to brotherhood and intercultural understanding! Hear here! (As mere Israelites—and total strangers at that—suing for the hand of a daughter of the dominant people, they had to offer an especially generous settlement. This included a big, big party—a week-long feast, paid for by Manoah, at the time of the wedding.)

Samson had a chance to talk with the girl now. Yes, polite, deferential, shy, a bit afraid of him. He liked that. She pleased him well. Tension grew.

On the way back to Dan, the family camped again at the same site, and Samson went off to look for the lion he'd killed. He'd thought about it all the time he'd been in Timnath, and he wanted to see it again. He found it largely picked apart by carrion, and a swarm of bees had made a hive of the chest cavity. Managing to grab a hunk of comb without too many stings, he ate, and he carried more back to the campsite for his parents. In the middle of this hard journey (travel was hard, the bargain had been hard, and reconciling themselves to their son's exogamy was especially hard), this unexpected treat delighted them. But their son evaded the question of where he'd found it, and they knew, from unpleasant past experience, not to press and irritate him when he chose not to tell them something. So they let it drop and just enjoyed the honey.

On the appointed day, Samson (tearing up the homestead the past few weeks, popping rivets and scorching everything he touched with the steam of his sexual energy) and Manoah (hoping, although uneasy about it, that marriage would help stabilize his son and set him more steadily on the path toward his destiny) returned to Timnath for the wedding. As per the deal, they hosted a week-long feast. Thirty young men of Timnath were among the feasters.

Finding himself in boisterous company with those filthy, uncircumcised Philistines, yet his spirits too high to start knocking their heads, he challenged them to a wager. In the middle of all the joking around on the first day of the feast, he said, "I've got a riddle."

Samson the Nazirite was, of course, perfectly sober, but his Timnite companions had been drinking a lot of Manoah's wine. Grinning, expecting a good bawdy one from the bridegroom, they said, "OK, yeah?"

"Not so fast. Let's make a bet. You guess the answer before the week's up, and I'll furnish each of you guys with a new bedsheet and a complete change of clothes—party favors for my dear guests. You don't guess, and you each owe me a sheet and a change of clothes. How's that?"

Caught up in a spirit of genial gamesmanship, spiked now with high-stakes aggression, they said, "Sure. Yeah. What the hell. Go ahead, ask us."

"OK, what am I describing? 'Out of the eater came forth meat, and out of the strong came forth sweetness.'"

"Hm, good one." So the young men of Timnath thought about it, discussed the possibilities with such clarity as the wine permitted. The riddle became a recurrent motif through the first few days of the feast: jokes on the first day, earnest deliberation on the second, and by the third day, frustration, as the Timnites feared they'd have to pay off the bet. Not only is he waltzing off with the prettiest girl in town AND her dowry, but he'll be making a little fortune in textiles, too. Sure, he throws a nice party, but he demands the shirt off your back. Who's getting the better end of this deal, anyway? Who does he think runs this country? You know they cut the foreskins off their little boys—mutilate their babies? These people are disgusting.

And so, the festive mood diminished. The wine, instead of uplifting the drinkers' spirits, twisted them.

A delegation of the young men paid the bride a little visit. She convinced them that Samson had not told her the answer to the riddle. OK, they said, then, um (delicate matter here, socially uncomfortable—how do you honorably speak to a married woman about her sex life?), did she think she might be able to *entice* the answer from her husband?

She blushed. She strove mightily to suppress a grin. Samson was the least delicate man she'd ever met—might as well ask her to work her eye-fluttering wiles against a typhoon. Coyness, games—all irrelevant before the muscular overmastery that would blast into the room and just take her. When he gripped her pelvis and shoved it against his own, it was, bizarrely, as though he wasn't aware of her presence there in the room with him.

"I really don't think that would work," her grin resisting all suppression.

One of the angrier young men: "You bring this guy in to take what we have, isn't that so? Make a deal with you: you find out the answer for us, and we won't burn down your father's house with you inside it. Deal?"

Deal it was. That night, after the bull had relaxed, she asked him the answer to his riddle. When Samson evaded, she said, "You hate me, don't you? You ask my people this riddle, and you don't even tell me the answer—your own wife!"

"Look, I haven't even told my parents. You think I'd tell you before I told them?"

The implied insult, the neighbors' threat to her own family—and a calculation that it just might work—all brought her to tears. She wept that night, she wept the next night, she wept whenever she was alone with her husband. This was not sexy. Those first days, his moments alone with her had been great, not only as a respite from his responsibility to play host to those filthy, uncircumcised louts, but also for the really satisfying sex. The way she would just submit totally, it made him feel an absolute power. He was God's instrument on Earth, Man of Destiny, as he took her little breasts into his mouth or slid his hands around her perfect little butt. He could whip her around any way he liked—no pause in the spontaneity (as had occurred in some of his previous sexual experiences) to negotiate a price for this or that position. She just did it. Now that was wifely duty.

But now, he couldn't even talk to this uncooperative little puddle of tears. How could they have any fun in bed with her constantly whimpering? She was so touchy. What did it matter whether she knew the riddle? He didn't get it. Maybe he just didn't understand women. Or maybe his parents were right: he shouldn't mix himself up with Philistine trash. If marriage was going to be like this, maybe he didn't want it after all. First thing to do, though, was to shut up all this blubbering. So he told her the story of the carrion-picked lion with the beehive. What did it matter, after all, if she knew? She might even come to admire him the more for his bravery in killing a lion. (Just a cub? Hey, an angry mama lion might have pounced from behind any rock.)

Ah, she hugged him tight and thanked him for this token of his faith in her. She became her sweet, compliant self again, but Samson had turned. He liked submissive, but he hated weak. All that crying: emotional blackmail for what seemed to him small gain. Why'd she care?

On the seventh day, before the sun went down, the young men of the city, shit-eating grins all over their smarmy faces, said to him, "What's sweeter than honey? What's stronger than a lion?"

The Man of Destiny said darkly, "If you hadn't plowed with my heifer, you'd never have dug that up." She'd been right: he hated her.

He'd lost the bet. The week-long party was over anyway, so he left. He didn't even stop to say good-bye to his new bride, just snuck off toward Ashkelon, another Philistine town. He did not, of course, have ready access to thirty sheets and thirty changes of clothes. That's why he went to Ashkelon. Even though the Timnites had cheated, *he* was an honorable man, and he would pay his debt. Using all his strength, stealth, and cunning, as well as a great, angry fund of adrenalin, he overpowered men out alone, invaded homes, stole bedsheets from wardrobes and clotheslines, killed men and undressed them, killed others who caught him thieving, and, after some dangerous weeks, came back to Timnath with full payment for his wager. He bragged to them that for each change of clothes he handed over, he'd killed a Philistine.

Samson left, returning to his father's house without even stopping to see his wife. He did not return for her. He sent no message. The girl's family assumed, after several months, that he had, in his rage, abandoned her. (Filthy Israelite—what can you expect from them anyway? A thief and a murderer. Who wants him?) So they married her off again to a nice young Philistine boy—in fact, the same one who had agreed, since Samson had brought none with him, to stand as best man at her first wedding. Her family was much happier with this match, and so was the bride. (The sex was more gentle. She liked that.)

Around the time of the wheat harvest, Samson's rage settled. All the hard work of bringing in the crop sweated it out of him, and he was now too tired by the end of each day to lie in his bed dreaming of spectacular revenge. He decided to return to Timnath, make peace, and take his wife home with him.

He arrived in town with a kid that he planned to slaughter to inaugurate a new era of reconciliation with his bride and her family. Samson walked up to the door where his father-in-law stood and told the man as much, then asked if he could enter his wife's chamber, hoping she'd forgive him and maybe, as a sign of reconciliation, have sex. (After all, they were married, and, well, it had been months.)

Her father: "Um," and a long pause. Not insensitive to Samson's likely perspective on this situation (legal spouse of a woman now, with her father's explicit approval, sleeping with another man, Samson might see his father-in-law as a particularly scandalous variety of pimp), he nonetheless recognized now that this willful Israelite might not have been the best match for his little girl. She was happy with this second husband, but the first had a claim that the father felt no organized society could ignore. What could he do?

Well, first of all, and with great apologies, he forbid Samson to enter the daughter's chamber. She had married someone else, and it would not do to allow her time alone with this man: not merely because it would *imply* scandalous intimacy but also because this fellow was likely to demand and expect sexual intimacy to which he was no longer entitled. But since, clearly, Samson assumed he was still so entitled, the father, as his second move, offered, in a spirit of proactive compromise, his second, even prettier daughter, as a substitute bride.

Though Samson rejected the offer, he took this whole exchange calmly. There before his father-in-law's house, he turned his face toward heaven, lifted the kid above his head, and said, "Praised be the name of the Lord! For now, I shall be more blameless than the Philistines in all my actions. Surely, my lust for this maiden came from God." And he turned away singing psalms of praise and vengeance to the god who had now given him reason to turn with fury upon the Philistines. The fire of lust that had begun the story had been lit by God himself to provoke Samson, in righteous anger, toward his destiny. Anything he might now do to the Philistines would manifest now not cruelty, but God's own justice.

He caught foxes on the hillsides round the town, tied torches to their tails, and let these animals, mad with fear and pain, run flaming through the standing wheat, flee their own tails into the shocks of harvested grain, dash into the vineyards and olive groves to die in the heat of the vines and trees they set ablaze. The foxes yelled unheard beneath the roar and crackle of the fires they set, too wild with pain for the Timnites to catch and douse to save their food. The foxes died amid the harvest, and the people of Timnath watched starvation blazing all around them. So Samson began his revenge.

Facing famine, all of Timnath turned upon the family they held responsible for this catastrophe. This family let this savage Israelite into their village and then provoked him by giving his wife to another man. Let them pay.

They surrounded the house, tossed firebrands through the windows and up into the roof thatch. As the family rushed out, the neighbors caught the father and elder daughter. Those two, they overpowered and tied to a rail, then heaved that rail into the flames—just as the young men at the wedding had threatened. The rest of the family, the town allowed to live, to return and settle in the ashes of their neighbors' vengeance. But who would ever share food now with the family responsible for the famine?

While the crowd milled around the still-burning house, Samson appeared at the end of the street. These people, he told himself, in subborning his wife, stole from him the happiness of his marriage, made him a thief and a murderer, all for the sake of a lousy wager. Praised be God for making even Philistine scum the instruments of his destiny. "Though you have done me this favor," he said, pointing to the ruin, "still I will have my revenge on you." So he rushed into the crowd with his blade drawn, slashing it into thighs and hips: severing arteries and nerves, cracking femurs. Then, before the Timnites could organize themselves, preoccupied as they were at first with the crippled and dying, Samson fled.

He fled to the top of the Rock of Etam, in Judah. A Philistine posse was organized, and they tracked him as far as Lehi, which is near Etam. The people of Judah naturally felt nervous seeing this contingent of armed Philistines camping out in their territory. So they sent a delegation to ask the reason their tribe was being honored by this visit.

"After this fellow Samson. Danite. Wanted for murder and robbery in Ashkelon, arson and murder in Timnath. Pretty near destroyed the whole town up there. I'm sure you heard of that. Came to pour the same medicine down his throat. What town you say you're from, son?"

The elders of Judah, eager to demonstrate their loyalty to their rulers, organized a posse of their own to haul Samson down from Etam. Three thousand men combed the great Rock till they cornered the fugitive. Then their captain came in to negotiate with him.

"I'm not going to hurt you," he said. "Just tell me why you're here. What's with you anyway? You forget the Philistines got us by the balls?" He spread his hands. "I'm not accusing you of anything at all, myself. But if you got some grudge against Judah that you want to get us in trouble, I'd like to know about it. Maybe I can set it straight."

"Eye for an eye. They did to me, I do to them."

"They burned your fields?"

"Come on, you know what I mean."

"Well, actually, no, I don't. And now I want you to stay very still. Don't make a move. You know I have a few dozen armed men right here. I'm going to take this rope and tie you up. You're under arrest."

"One thing."

"Sure."

"You're going to hand me over? OK, I understand. Just promise me you won't kill me yourselves. Fellow Israelites."

"Fellow Israelites. You got it, bud."

Uneasy about what they were doing (after all, they didn't like those filthy, uncircumcised Philistines, either), the men from Judah tied up Samson with two brand new ropes, led him down from the rock, and marched him at spearpoint over to Lehi.

As the Philistines saw the Israelite posse approach, with the fugitive tied up and helpless, they started yelling anti-Israelite slogans: things about pigs and circumcisions. And they ridiculed the failed Israelite ambition to rule over this whole country—given the Philistine dominion in the South for over a generation now, clearly a failure. If anybody's going to massacre the native peoples and take their land, the Philistines bragged, it's going to be us. In the meantime, who's under whose thumb, eh?

Samson couldn't take it anymore. As he approached, he saw them make lewd gestures with their daggers and shout his name. That provided him the adrenal rush he needed to snap his ropes (ill-made? untested? poorly tied?). He burned now, and his bonds were like flax in his flame. Free, he grabbed for a weapon. His captors sprung away—he was dangerous, a rabid beast in their ranks. No blade came to his hand, so he lunged for the roadside, where a dead donkey lay, and he tore the jawbone out of its well-decayed sockets—a blunt scythe with teeth that cut.

He charged, yelling prayers and curses. Oblivious to his countrymen, he slammed his jawbone into the heads and ribs of any Philistine he caught—helpless before his mad strength. He would smash at a man till he was sure his skull had cracked, then grab another. So intent on his bloody work, so single-mindedly hateful, he didn't see he'd led his countrymen into a battle. He noticed each individual death he caused and focused his attention on the next filthy, uncircumcised Philistine within his grasp, but could not broaden his vision toward the overall victory he inspired. One enormous victory at a time, man by man, the great breadth of a human soul would fall under his arm. In hand to hand combat, nothing larger is imaginable.

Emerging, in exhaustion, from his berserk trance, he saw the field around him taken by the sons of Judah. Or had it been (his mind still smoldered) by himself alone? "I have killed my thousand," he reeled. "Am I to die now from thirst? Help me. I'll fall into the hands of my enemies," who lay now horizontal all around him. He knelt and pounded his bloody jawbone on a rock in delusional anger at the irony. It broke in two as one of his former captors, now companions, rushed water to him. And he dipped the hollow of the bloody, moldy, decayed jawbone of a dead donkey—the bone he'd just been using to kill people—into the leather sack to ladle himself a sip of water. Ah, sweetest water ever. Who needs wine?

2.

Samson became a hero to the cause of Israelite independence, an unofficial leader and judge for his people under the loose yoke of Philistine rule. So long as the Philistines received their tribute regularly, their leaders did not generally interfere in the internal affairs of the Israelite communities—waste of time. So if these people turned to Samson to settle their disputes among one another, fine. In fact, judicial duties might keep that well-known troublemaker productively distracted. Sure, he was a thorn, but an all-out campaign to capture him wouldn't be worth the expense and probable loss of life. Let him be.

So for about twenty years, Samson judged his people, made anti-Philistine speeches, and when the urge overwhelmed him, snuck into Philistine cities to visit their prostitutes. He still couldn't bring himself to sleep with the pure sisters of Israel, and the danger of sneaking in among his enemies heightened the excitement of those sexual encounters. And the slaughter of Philistines that followed from his marriage to one of them convinced him that his attraction to Philistine women was divinely inspired and would lead him on to still greater accomplishments.

Only once in all those years was he really in danger. While he was sleeping one night with a woman in the Philistine city of Gaza, her pimp, in an attempt to ingratiate himself with the righteous citizens who were prone to look down upon his profession, let it be known that Samson, the notorious Israelite agitator, was in a particular house with one of his girls. So a band of righteous citizens incensed at this Israelite pervert invading their community to corrupt the flower of Philistine womanhood, along with some of the pimp's local customers (actually, the two groups overlapped considerably), decided to wait for him at the city gates. They'd grab him in the morning as he tried to slip out the only entrance to the city— which, in peacetime, now remained unlocked and open all night. Anti-Israelite bigotry mixed with lingering resentment over his infamous attacks on peaceful, law-abiding Philistines. A good lynching ought to teach those barbarians respect for authority. But Samson, ever wary of the danger that spiced his erotic interludes, rose at midnight to avoid detection, slinked past the sleeping ambuscade, and carefully, slowly, quietly removed the lockbolt from the great gate as a trophy of his close escape. What a rush.

But that near miss was an exception. The years rolled by in a fairly satisfactory, perfectly peaceful way. He got to play the great man as people brought their cases before him, he got to vent his hatred against the Philistines in fiery speeches whenever he could gather a crowd, and his appetite for Philistine poontang remained undimmed. What more could a man ask?

At one point, he was living with a Philistine woman, Delilah. He liked her because she was open to all kinds of sexual experimentation—didn't just permit him to do things to her, but actually initiated a lot of original little games. To his surprise, Samson found bondage delightful. The game of Israelite Hero at the Mercy of His Philistine Captress turned him on like nothing he'd ever known. Playing at surrender, resisting as long as he could her demand that he come, then finally offering up his semen against his will—feeling his body defy and wrest control from his voluntarily shackled will—he could feel mind and body snap apart in obliterating bliss.

To maintain the game's piquancy, of course, they had to ratchet up the intensity from time to time. Needles pricked him with punishment; women's clothing offered him the thrill of humiliation. Samson, however, always laid out or approved the script for each session of his debasement, always maintained ultimate control over his own domination. He could always stop the game if the shout of pressing business came to his door or if he sensed his mistress pushing the game out from the secure realm of irony and play toward the border of straightforward cruelty. When she would feel a surge of power, erotic heat, she'd be tempted, but since her own satisfaction, too, lay in the obliteration of her own will into the structure of the game, she swallowed it, let the tension of suppressed lust for cruelty increase the internal pressure toward her own climax. Outside the game, she might indulge her own desire by imagining scenarios, but the rules were such that she might play them out only by first submitting them to the approval of her lover. For her, erotic tension always began with the anxious curiosity of proposal: would he approve of her hot candle wax idea and play it out with her, or would he reject it? Yes: tension and desire leap, to be compressed and denied in the game itself till they tear through the tissue of role playing into a real orgasm. No: disappointment sublimates into cruel imagination to construct, in retaliation for that denial, a revenge he might accept and allow her to play out upon his body. Which will it be? In the moment of proposal, she could gush with an eroticism that the game itself would channel tightly. Also, her people hated the Israelites with the same passionate bigotry the Israelites felt toward them. In a world where young women held few options for self-expression, she had distinguished herself with the outrageous transgression of living with a leader of Israel.

In the meantime, sick of Samson's blustery but, so far, fruitless anti-Philistine agitation, the lords of Gaza commissioned a band of warriors to go kidnap him. Who knows, after all, when this windbag might manage to blow embers of resentment into a real, flaming rebellion? Since he was, famously, the strongest man in Israel, they approached Delilah to assist them.

"All we ask," they said when they found her alone one day, "is you find out his weakness, the source of his strength."

"Why should I do this for you? I'm happy with him."

"Loyalty to your nation, patriotism."

Not a dent.

"We have been authorized to offer you as much as three hundred pieces of silver."

Ka-ching!

"One thing."

"Sure."

"I'll help you catch him, but please tell me you won't kill him. Please. I couldn't bear that."

"Could always use another slave. Sure, we won't kill him." And she settled her conscience on a nicely cushioned purse.

So next chance she had, she asked, under the guise of enhancing their erotic play, what was the source of his famous strength. "Oh, Samson! You're so big and strong!" He had just enough ironic sensibility to chuckle at that, but he loved it. "Wouldn't it be fun."

"What?"

"What if I."

"What?"

She giggled. "When I tie you up, you just pretend you can't get away. What if I really tied you down sometime? What if you couldn't get away? Den I coult schtomp you gudt, you badt boy."

Game to consider it, he fondled in his mind the psycho-sexual possibilities. "Yeah."

"Great!" She wilted with gratitude. "All right, so what makes you so strong? I could key in on that when I bind you."

God's will, he thought. Destiny, divinely decreed. My parents' vow. How do you get a rope around those things?

"I don't know," answering not her question but the one in his head. "Maybe some fresh green willow branches, still green, so they're still strong. Maybe that'll work. Maybe get six or seven long ones. Tie me down with that, and I'll be helpless as anybody."

When she passed that suggestion along to the Philistines, they assumed the willow held a magic to counteract whatever sorcery gave Samson his strength.

And so by the end of the day, they supplied Delilah with seven (mystical number) long, supple willow branches. Then they hid in Delilah's bedroom: a couple in the closet, two more behind a curtain in one corner, another below a trapdoor covered by a throw rug. The legend of Samson's strength and brutality had grown so vast over the twenty years since the disaster of his marriage that, even with the Israelite tied up, five to one felt like just barely a safe ratio.

That evening, the couple entered the room where the five spies hid. (Before they had handed over the willow, they had bathed—one of the tricks twelfth-century B.C.E. spies carried up their sleeves so that musky human funk would not render hiding places transparent.) The spies listened.

Mumbles and playful laughter, then, "Down, Israelite dog! On your back!" Then they heard the rustle of the branches, an occasional grunt or "ow" during the tying. Now, the sort of bondage game Samson and Delilah played lacked the black-leather sophistication of our modern editions. After all, they had stumbled on the game by accident, not out of the sexual boredom that seeks unimaginable sensual fulfillment in some model of decadence. Their culture had no received images to simmer in their imaginations such as the Prussian dominatrix with riding crop and boots. Without, say, some impossibly corrupt idea of Berlin in the 20s for them to aspire to (roles: besotted son of enervated Junkerdom, Valkyrie maiden contemptuous of the presuming worm), they had no fetishized elsewhere or elsewho they must emulate, no mere reflection of somebody else's perfect sexual intensity. They played roles, sure, but they weren't just playing somebody else playing a role.

So Samson and Delilah arranged the preliminaries of their unsophisticated fun, testing the branches and discussing knots. The Philistines in hiding had no idea what was going on. Some part of the magic of the willows? How'd she get him to cooperate? They just waited for their cue.

She had him all tied down. He was ready for the teasing, stroking, ball tickling that it was now his role to resist, resist, oh, to resist.

"Samson! The Philistines! At the door! I hear them!" This was not in the script. Fight! He strained, broke, broke, tore, snap, smack, broke … and … broke the bonds and jumped through the door brandishing a lampstand. Nobody's there.

The spies remained still.

To pre-empt his anger, "You lied to me. The willows are nothing. Flax in a fire. You mock me. Shithead. Don't care about my pleasure at all, do you? Why do you lie to me? Israelites! Why'd I get mixed up with such a bum anyway?"

Swirl in Samson's head: sexual excitement, fear, anger, embarrassment. "But Honeycup…." She glared at him, fuming rage, sweating her malevolence. What a turn on. So he picked her up, and they fucked with abandon.

The spies remained still, just listened, getting hard and uncomfortable while their cue to attack, unlike the two lovers, never did come.

Next day, she said, "OK, so willow branches don't work. Anything else that might?"

Samson, still game, forgiving her for the deception (after all, she just wants the tying up to work for real): "How about new ropes, never been used for any work?"

Same deal: spies, new rope, ties him to the bed. This time, she started in on the teasing. She'd found it pretty exciting to have an audience last night, and so she felt sorely tempted to get it on with Samson again and give those creeps another show. The spies themselves were torn between duty, acute embarrassment, and hard-ons like they'd never suffered before. Seemed like anything that happened tonight would satisfy them one way or another.

Ultimate teasing now: just as she began to lower herself onto his cock, "Oh, Samson! I hear them! They're after you!"

"Philistines?" The rage of sexual excitement—ready, if only he could, to grab her by the hips and plunge in—clicked to sheer neck-snapping violence, bypassing all memory or thought. Kill. Off at the edge of Samson's awareness, the rope tore as he rushed to the street. Nobody. She did it again? Just tested him?

This time, she tried a gentler chiding, wanting to put on another show again anyway, since she seemed to have the opportunity now. "Come on back to bed. You don't want to tell me? I understand. You need to keep something private, and this is important to you. It's OK. Come back to bed, and ... I'll make you feel better." She sat on the edge of the bed, massaged his penis and kissed his belly. One of his hands groped downward to fondle her breasts and pinch her nipples, and the other pushed her head downward toward his crotch. The spies in a position to do so risked peeping through the chinks in their camouflage. The one suffocating under the carpeted trap had scrunched himself (none too comfortably) so that he'd have a hand ready between his thighs this time, and he gently, silently rubbed himself to the rhythms of the goings-on above him.

"Mm, Samson."

"Mm." Pushed at her head, but she spoke again, keeping her hand pumping.

"Your strength." Lick. "Where does it come from?"

"Oh."

Hand stops. "Where does it come from? I want to finish you. Tell me." Another slow, languorous, drippy lick. Then away. She grabbed it again and looked him in the eye. "Tell me."

"I."

"Yes?" Pump.

"Will you?"

"Yes." Slow stroke. She could feel him tensing toward climax now. Needed to hold back just right. "Yes." Her mouth again.

Like a bull busting a weak gate to the cow pasture, he slammed through a barrier in his mind. "My," yes! "hair!" yes!

And then everybody, one way or another, felt greatly relieved.

At breakfast, she asked, "Your hair? You mean, like, if I tie you up by your hair, you'd lose your strength?"

"Hah! Tie it to the roofbeam, and I'll carry the roof away. That's not what I meant." And he just dismissed her inquiries about what he meant, regretted giving in even as far as he had.

"You're just kidding me: 'willow,' 'new rope,' 'hair.' Every day, you tell me a new lie. You love me?"

"Yes, Honeycup, you know I do."

"Oh, yeah? How can you say you love me when you hide things? Tell me the secret. Me of all people. Who knows your body better? You just don't care."

And for the next three days she badgered him, wore him down till he started to feel she wasn't much fun anymore. For his own peace of mind, he half wanted to break up with her, but he'd had with her the best sex in his life. What a dilemma. But she got to be a one-note conversationalist. And this whine was souring her musical voice. She snarled at him. He snarled back. Cold shoulder repelled cold shoulder in their bed at night. She greeted him in the morning, "Hair, huh? Hah!" Am I just being stubborn? he asked himself. Is it really worth it? Is it right to conceal my devotion to God? Is a dried up sex life my punishment? So he convinced himself that a frank conversation about his privileged place in sacred history would help his love life.

He explained to Delilah the Nazarite vow his parents had initiated for him (the ban on haircuts and grapes, the sense of destiny), and he credited that for his great strength. Since God granted him this power to use against Philistines, her calls to defend himself against them had only fueled it, no matter how he was bound. "So probably nothing will work."

"Grapevines?"

"Uh, let's not try it."

So, as she understood his bizarre lecture on weird Israelite religious practices, this lifelong Nazarite vow worked a kind of magic, and he apparently feared a grapevine could break it. So a haircut might break the spell, too. Though Samson, on one hand, had stressed his role in the destiny of God's chosen people and the piety of such outward signs of fealty as the long hair, what she, on the other hand, heard was a magic spell she could cut with a razor.

Later that day, she contacted the Philistines and told them he had finally revealed the source of his strength. They handed her the money and arranged to lie in wait again for him that night.

That night, she made up with him, offered him his favorite meal, massaged his tense muscles, had him fall asleep with his head in her lap. Once again, they were at peace with one another. The spies were disappointed that they didn't get a sex show this time, but they waited silently for their cue. When Samson had entered the deepest stage of sleep, she motioned for one of the spies. He emerged from behind the curtain, and he produced a razor. The spy had no intention of— as you might expect, even despite his promise to Delilah—slitting the Israelite hero's throat. Too convinced that Samson's power lay in his hair, he didn't think a cut elsewhere would work. As instructed, he shaved the sleeper.

Bald.

Delilah shouted, "Samson! The Philistines!"

He jumped up, saw one right in front of him. No lie this time. Guy has a razor. Watch out, he'll cut me. Looks around for a weapon, sees hair all over the floor. Touches his head. Both hands.

"Woman!"

But everyone in the room, including Samson, who should have known better, was now convinced of his weakness. The other four Philistines emerged from hiding, and Samson let them bind him up, in ropes he would have torn apart the day before. When they'd secured him, the barber-spy took his razor and slit the hero's eyes. Samson tasted the salty fluid running into his mouth as he bawled—as he felt the pain sear away the very root of his strength. He collapsed into manageable helplessness. Quickly, a gag into his mouth, and they slipped him out of Dan.

They took him to Gaza, shackled him and put him in a workhouse where, as a strong slave, his duty was now to turn the millwheel that ground the city's grain. Blind now, he was perfectly docile. Unlike people who have been blind for years, the newly sightless Samson had not yet learned how to sense the positions of people and objects, so he couldn't strike at his captors or escape. Helpless, demoralized, mourning his light, he submitted. His lust for a Philistine woman had not, it seemed, come from God who wished to lead him thereby toward destiny. That assumption was, he saw now, hubris, sheerest self-delusion. Loving the dirtiness of it all, he'd scattered his seed on ground he knew to be cursed, rather than used it to extend God's healthy plantation of Israel. Destined from his conception a leader of God's own people, hailed by them as their Judge to maintain the peace and unity of the holy nation, he had squandered his destiny on a few lousy humps in the mattress. He felt disgusted. To dumbly, blindly circle round a dusty mill till the end of his days struck him as a perfectly just punishment. He deserved no better.

(Note: slaves get no wine, and hair grows back.)

The lords of the Philistines were, of course, delighted. The chief agitator among their Israelite subjects, "The Strongest Man in Israel," was neutralized, humiliated. This blind slave would be a sign of their dominion. His capture had roused Philistine patriotism. Nobody is big enough and bad enough to kick around the Philistines! We gonna kick some Israelite butt! Woof!

So at the feast to Dagon, chief of the Philistine gods, the leaders of Gaza had Samson called out of his workhouse to become a visible sign of Philistine power. He was to be put on display for public humiliation. Samson, they calculated, would serve as a useful device for controlling the Philistine populace. Here they had an official enemy, actual murderer of Philistines, rabble-rousing rebel against their legitimate authority, a guy who had been spouting hatred against them for two decades. If they could keep public resentment focused on this official enemy, if they could keep discontent focused on this sign of an external and internal Israelite threat, then internal restiveness would turn toward the political leadership for protection rather than against it in rebellion. The feast of Dagon was an excellent occasion to exploit the propaganda potential in their prize war trophy.

So they had a boy lead Samson into the great hall of the palace. That the "Great Hero" of Israel would need such a feeble guard was part of the humiliation—humiliation that was now no longer a game he controlled. Samson understood what was happening and, in his depressive state, felt he deserved it all: the hisses and the pelting with spoiled food.

Desire for their women, for their abominations, led me here. Showed I but restraint, I'd not be here. I'd touch not vinestock, but I'd dip my prick in rancid pussy. I am not worthy. I have befouled my mother's oaths for me, and my lusts have led me here, into this pit of uncleanliness. No truly faithful Nazarite in mind nor body, I have been unclean since first I cracked a pagan twat—no, earlier, when first I felt a warm rise at the thought of Gentile girls in other valleys. Since first I sprouted fuzz, I've been a hypocrite. All my hatred, all my patriotism, all my love of Jacob's god—all of it, at base, my lowest carnality, perverted heavenward. Desire to fuck their women led me here. I am not worthy. Lord, have mercy on my wretched soul. I am not as I imagined that I was. I am not worthy. Lord, have mercy on my wretched soul. I have been violent; I have been lustful. Lord, I am not worthy of the honors I've received.

And Samson experienced a new sensation then: humility.

Desire for their whores has led me here. Desire for their whores led me into the snare. Desire to fuck their whores led me into vanity at the gates of Gaza. Desire for their whores led me into hiding at the Rock of Etam. Desire to fuck their whores led me even to marry one. And for that, I starved and killed them.

The growing banquet sounds then widened as he entered through the doorway, and roared then louder as they recognized him—anger, laughter, clapping. I deserve this. I betrayed my vows.

"Where am I?"

The boy said, "Municipal banquet hall. The King's guests are eating, and all that can fit have been invited to watch."

"Them eat?"

"That too."

And me, the captive freak. Desire to spurt into their whores has led me here. Whence this perverse desire? What made me some kind of ethnic pervert? Lord, how could you?

The boy tugged on his armchains, lifting one to left, and one to right.

"What's this?"

"Chaining you to these pillars. Middle of the hall so everyone can see."

And so he cogitated. Now, wait a minute.

Chains tightened, and his upper body pulled taut, already an inviting target for garbage to splat and thump against his chest.

I married one, and that brought me into their town. I murdered Philistines to pay off that bet, got her family and village destroyed, and then led a battle that killed more filthy, uncircumcised Philistines. What more righteous work for a godly man? God led me by my sins to do his work, pointed me by the hard-on toward my mission.

Splat on the cheek, something ripe and juicy.

At the Lord's beckoning, I entered this building through Delilah's filthy hole, and now I am here to fulfill His holy will.

"Boy."

"Yeah?"

"Can you get me a cup of water?"

"Sure, why not."

And off he goes. Wait. Wait.

By the ends of his fingers, he caressed the stone.

God is great. Desire to fuck their women comes from his inscrutable good will. And he pulled.

Great stones crushed his enemies. A great stone ripped his body from his soul.

JEPHTHAH
JUDGES 11-12

After the main events of this story, Jephthah became a bitter and a fierce judge, not just a scourge to the unrighteous, but a cat-o'-nine-tails, complete with a flesh-tearing hook at the end of each line that would grip in past skin and into muscle, its wielder's job not just to lash, but to pull, to yank the hooks through, drawing more than blood—bits of meat—and from the greened meat adhering from the last day's flogging to leave behind infections that would lingeringly kill. A hanging judge takes grim pride and pleasure in delivering his justice. Jephthah did not. He had lost all delight.

For instance, when the men of the tribe of Ephraim raided unsuccessfully into Gilead hoping to viking away the booty from the Ammonite war, he authorized this reprisal: at the ford across the Jordan, stop individually each man as he crosses. Do not harm any innocent non-Ephraimite who might be about some legitimate business.

So a young man of Ephraim gone a-plundering would find himself drawn aside from other crossers at the river's edge—the sacred Jordan toward his home. A profitable pillage upon Gilead with all the exciting fun of rape, slaughter, and treasure (an adolescent and comic-book vision of power and potency) became, suddenly, frightening.

They are strong after all, and I, a rabbit aquiver in the grass as the hawk descends.

"What's this?"

Non sequitur. The gear shift dulls whatever sharpness fear imparted to his wits. Polite young man, he answers the innocent question put to him. "A wheatstalk." And then he feels the bladeshaft from behind him, and then he feels nothing else ever again.

To another: "What's this?"

"Wheatsaft."

"Wheatshaft."

"What I said: *sibboleth.*"

"*Shibboleth.*"

Blade deep into the back, between his ribs.

Ephraimite accent done him in.

Jephthah, as I said, took from it neither satisfaction nor sorrow. Nor did his bitterness increase. It lay already deep as a human soul may plumb.

Does the story of his daughter explain his cruelty? No.

Once upon a time, the elders of Gilead prevailed upon the famous outlaw Jephthah to defend them from the Ammonites who raided across the border, torching barns and homes, carrying away their livestock, women, and slaves. "And you shall become Judge over us, like Gideon and Deborah before you."

They appealed to his ambition. They appealed to his pocketbook. They appealed to his posterity, for his daughter, his only child, would need a husband soon, and for that, respectability would help. They appealed to him on account of his cunning and brutality, and on account of the rage that they knew boiled within him and that he'd learned to channel into the leadership and profit of the thugs who followed him.

"I see my brothers here among you."

He saw that they appealed also, without directly saying so, to his sense of magnanimity. Here is your chance to show that you are a better man than they are, more generous, forgiving, open-hearted.

"You need not fear me." He thus accepted especially that final, unstated offer from the sons of his father's wives. "My father protected me, his firstborn child while he lived. Now I shall protect you." The authority in those words was his revenge.

This was a lot for the brothers to take from the whore's son they'd banished. It's a measure of their desperation that they took it.

"Deal?"

Yeah, OK, sure, deal.

"All right. Good thing you guys came to me. First thing I learned in my line of work: violence is not necessary. Nine times out of ten, my associates and I walk up to some lone traveler or isolated farmhouse—if we ask them politely for their money, they give it to us." To their skeptical eyes, "Really, a polite request is the way to start. Save everybody a lot of trouble."

Hired themselves a good axe-swinging barbarian, and what do they get? Some white-shoed diplomat.

Tedious back and forth of messengers about the legalities of who owned the land. ("Is not." "Is so." "Nuh-uh." "Yeah-huh.")

Jephthah: "Got them right where we want them now, boys. Gird your loins, and let's head on out!"

Only the thugs Jephthah had brought with him made any move.

Suspecting a trap. I soldier off into battle, and they're down one outlaw. "You guys OK?"

"It's, well, it's this diplomacy thing."

"Diplomacy thing." Walking purposefully toward them, straight into the face of the skinny guy up front, "You think I don't know what I'm doing, that it?"

"No, no, that's not it. It's just that—"

Jephthah came in close. Pick another one. Little guy. This is good. Bear down upon him, get his nose in my barbarian funk. My stench tells him, you can smell how much more a man I am than you. I mean right in his face—nose on nose, garlic breath right into mouth, awl-sharp eyes punching little holes into the other guy's pupils. "You don't think I know what I'm doing."

"No, of course not. I just—"

"You hired me to do a job—"

"Yes, and we—"

The little guy—how could Jephthah know?—had led the most silent livestock raids on Caananite pastures. No one ever heard a thing—maybe one slit-throat shepherd for just a moment—till, in the morning, nothing bleated. An intimidated step back covered a movement of his knife hand.

"You—," back to the skinny one, didn't know the turn had saved him.

Squeak: "Me?"

"—don't think I mean it. Do you?"

"Course I—"

"You don't think I mean it." Will welled in him now, muscling out any doubts in himself, shoving weakling uncertainty aside and lunging forward toward some great meaty beast, spear tip pointed toward the heart, toward eyes he could will to a frightened stillness. "I tell you what I'm going to do." Hand on the skinny guy's shoulder now, kneading it with a gentle I-can-snap-your-clavicle intimacy.

The guy's eyes darting toward his friend with the knife, who nods.

"Look at me! You're the ones who wanted me here." Looked around at them all, "To show you how much I'm committed now to your cause—your cause—when I get back—having beat those fuckers, I might add, to a chewy pulp—"

"Hyah!" from his own men, some tentatively raised fists from a few others.

"(You still don't really believe in me, do you?) I...."

They're leaning in. They really do want to know.

Quietly, "Shall perform a sacrifice."

Whew. They all settled back. Big deal. Standard procedure.

"First thing I see when I come home. Let the Lord himself decide."

OK, now they're impressed. This is a gamble, big one—could be anything from a dove landing on a fencepost to that bull he's so proud of. Well, all right then. Here's your heedless barbarian, now.

As one: "Hyah!"

Hope it is the bull, Jephthah thought. Yeah, show I'm serious. "OK, let's make this official." He raised his face toward the sky, stood to his full height, and spread his arms wide, palms up. Shouting, as though to a tall and deaf man, "O Lord!" And the presumption suddenly scared him: "If you should," but he recovered, "without fail deliver into my grip not just the fighting men, but the little children of Ammon as well, I shall break them. And when I return in peace, then whatever—" breaks contact with the sky. Wide, his eyes look at some of the men around him, but not at his brothers, then back up, wide still, "—whatever walks out the door of my house to meet me shall be the Lord's, and I will offer it up for a burnt offering!"

"Did he say, 'door'?"
"He said, 'door.'"
"'Door'?"
"That's what he said."

And it was a glorious slaughter: Ammonite dead littered across the plain like beer cups across a post-game stadium, blood on everybody's hands like over-dolloped mustard, not only Israelite towns returned, but also twenty Ammonite towns along with their vineyards taken; a gratifying wail of widows and howl of orphans as they heard the news from the battlefront or else either witnessed or fled from the village-square executions; the exhaustion and terror of the survivors' evacuation toward they knew not what refugee welcome—likely, instead of welcome, blame for the loss of the little kingdom's western march. They would starve.

Jephthah had a lot to feel proud of: an exemplary demonstration of force. Divine blessing had definitively come to rest upon the brow of the outlaw bastard. The sins, he thought, of my mother, the sins that are my own: the Lord does not disdain us for them, but He forgives and adds a blessing gift beyond our hopes. He was tearing with joy, a swelling heart, and the manly happy countenances of all his fellows, the cool clean sweetness of the Jordan as he crossed back homeward, birdsong, and the calm clear pure sky. The Lord's own world is good, and He has given us dominion within it. I owe Him. No, I give Him freely, and more, whatever He Himself shall ask. One happy, large-spirited barbarian.

And with his lieutenants—his thief companions now men of rank along with Gileadite yeomen of long standing—he topped the rise before his onetime hideout, now his ranch. "There it is, my friends. And the Lord shall send us now an oracle of how I am to honor His triumph."

And as befit the leader's joyful mood, rattling a tambourine, his daughter danced out of the homestead to greet them. Happy for her daddy, sure, but the hero's daughter can expect a better marriage deal than can the daughter of—well, the sort of man her dad had been. She dreamed of a happily ever after and a prince.

She saw her father lift his face and shout: a joy of an intensity she's never seen before in anyone. She saw his shoulders go back and his knees fold, and his body fell beyond horizontal backwards. And the thump of his head on the road neither deadened nor spiked his scream as it, incredibly on that same initial breath, increased its volume on a smooth-sloped crescendo. Then all his joints collapsed, and flat he lay as a stalking lion in the grass. And then he was quiet.

He saw nothing but the sky. The empty blue.

As he drew a breath to cry again, his lieutenants saw his daughter's eyes sharpen and her mouth slack. And all her body language shifted from around and around to forward, straight downhillward (the tambourine she dropped rolled jangling and singing down the slope), over the fence toward her father.

"The ram."

"I saw it too."

"Through the gate."

"The ram came through the gate."

Empty blue.

"He—"

Shrugs, dumb looks, and shaking heads.

He couldn't even say her name. Sunlight. Sunlight. Now faces shade me.

She: my face shades his. "Daddy."

Then he drew a large and dignified breath, raised himself up. Did not look at her as he perfunctorily dusted himself off—not fastidiousness, but delay. "Daughter." He looked at her, and his barbaric mug melted into a weeping. He put his hands up to his collar, and he tore. Frayed threads and chest hair: signs of grief. "Alas!" Our twenty-first century English has no equivalent for it. "Alas! My daughter, you have brought me low!" The unconscious, in anger, does its wonted switcheroo, attaching itself to the object at hand. "You're one of those against me now." And then his anger switched back inward. "I have opened my mouth unto the Lord, and I cannot go back." He banished his conscious, deliberate mind. He had a commission to fulfill.

"Father, if you swore," with Antigone intensity, "we'll have to do it." Her certainty calmed him. The narrative she entered now gave her purpose. I shall become a legend. "Forasmuch as the Lord has taken vengeance for you of your enemies."

Who, he wondered, is my enemy?

"I only ask one thing."

"Yours."

"Two months with my friends. We'll go camping in the mountains." Toward the horizon, "I'll never marry now."

"Let it be."

And so they settled down for a long meditation upon the nature of tragedy.

"Tell him about the ram."

"You want to tell him about it?"

"You tell him."

"No, you tell him about it."

"No, you."

This is how they arranged it. She and her friends packed clothes. They got a tent and other supplies, including wool to spin so they wouldn't be completely idle. Weekly, a flunky with a donkey brought them food. They had a pleasant hilly acreage: a lot of rocks, not many trees for shade, some grass between the rocks. A more densely populated country would use this land to pasture goats or grow olives. Israel still settled sparsely on these hills. The girls would have a large, un-peopled place all to themselves.

Jephthah set a guard discretely round a broad perimeter. The girls would feel they were safe, out of the reach of any men, even—or especially—the guards.

This setting of the guard presented Jephthah with a problem. Not the logistics of setting a guard—he knew how to do that. Here's the question: how well should they guard her?

Not that he didn't want his daughter safe: of course he did. Since her mother had died and since he had no other children, she was his only. Without her, he knew, he had no future. All was in those pretty eyes and dancer limbs. Her laugh, her kitchen skill—how proud he felt of the things she'd learned to do with lamb and chickpeas. So worthy of a good man's protection.

Without her, I have no future. I who should have been her stay against all danger, I whose great role was to protect her through a childhood until I found a good young man to bear that role throughout the rest of life or till strong sons of her own could take it up, I have failed—not only failed her, but become the very author of her harm. Potential harm. (Not a depressive by nature, he couldn't give in to despair, but permitted himself still an angry hope.)

She and her friends, protect them well. In his own experience of outlawry, he knew their danger. How might he and his associates have responded to the news of young women on the cusp of nubility alone on a hill? (Shame, pleasure, horror, and fear collided in his memory. Why had they been there? Outside the law, one must seize opportunity. Enjoyed them through their tears and then sold them as slaves.) They must be guarded well by men he trusted, men who would watch one another.

"Sure, boss, I understand. Nobody gets inside the perimeter. We know how to do that. Count on it." Pause, well-rehearsed contraction of the brow. Delicate point. "But should we let anyone outside it?"

"Hm?"

"Which way should we look?"

Outside it. Let them go. Let her run away, and my problem evaporates. I can't kill a daughter I do not have. Ask the boys to turn their vigilance one direction.

"Boss—"

"I'm thinking."

This is impious. I have sworn an oath. But isn't it vanity to care about my honor before my daughter's life? If I let them leave— Them? Her only? Rape. Slavery. My mother the whore, only likelihood for an outcast woman. But a life. Would I wish my daughter such a life? I would be honor-bound (vanity again) to end it. Cleansing sacrifice in any case.

How to let her know she can go? In two months, she could figure it out. I am being untrue to my oath. I couldn't tell her. Can I have this guy suggest it? Not let her know it came from me? The Lord will know I am untrue. Even instructions to the guards, even hints dropped would be a betrayal. They must all discern it for themselves. Guards and girls.

And they may not.

"Don't tempt me. This is impious. I swore an oath."

"Sure thing. Whatever you say." Backing down.

"And are you suggesting," willfully working up a bit of anger, an emotion in which he felt more comfortable, "my daughter would act so disloyally?"

"No, just presenting an option, just throwing it out there. And you've rejected it. Issue settled."

Issue settled. He wasn't sure he wanted it to be. "If she would—"

"Issue settled, boss. You're absolutely right. In a pastoral society, there is no role for an unmarried woman." Slavery and prostitution he would not mention.

Best she can do, Jephthah knew, is to find the bed of a powerful man, as my mother found the bed of my father. But it was life at his pleasure, and it included the scorn of his wives and their sons. And always the concubine's bright, pleasing face toward her master—not entirely false, for he had given her a home and acted kindly toward her boy. My father must have known the blade-sharp jealousies among the women, but my mother always made him feel he was the great, bright pleasure of her life, and that silky flattery so soothed him he didn't seem to feel much need to investigate the desperation (fear of the slave shacks, fear of the wilderness, fear of the wives) that lay behind it. A powerful man is prone to vanity, and hint of resentment toward his concubine brought out the protective patriarch in him. Treating his bastard on equal terms with his legitimate sons increased the sons' resentment against the boy and thus made the satisfaction he took in his protective magnanimity all the greater. He felt his power within the home in being the boy's protector. But for me, he thought, they would gouge my child's eyes out and leave him in the desert. Jephthah's mother died, and but for the gouging, when his father died, that's what they did. Lucky for Jephthah, he'd fallen in with thieves.

"But listen, if she—"

"Gotcha, boss. Say no more."

Got what? Have I betrayed the Lord already? These men shall know my shame.

"No."

"As you wish it."

I don't even know what I said no to. What does he mean?

I wish upon a brave and handsome prince to rescue this my damsel in distress.

Jephthah's daughter stood a little apart from her three friends—maybe out of earshot, maybe not. In the sunlight on that shadeless hill, the rocks shone white, the tall grass between them stood, in the breezeless air, in vivid strips of green, and the sky domed high over all, a cloudless blue.

"Oh," with a sigh, said the most worshipful of her three friends, "she's so tragic!" And the object of her admiration straightened her spine and saddened her eyes for a self-consciously tragic pose. "We've got to do something for her."

"You mean go with her?" said the friend who was most freaked-out scared by the whole business. "Or just help her escape?"

"Yeah," the third, "it's not that we're, like, guards here or anything. He is."

He stood farther off than Jephthah's daughter herself. The guy was a pro; officially speaking, he neither heard nor saw. He suspected this discussion of escape was one of the things he was not officially to notice. The lieutenant's lifted eyebrow and judicious nod had suggested the guard was supposed to understand his instructions without being told. He pretended he understood that wink at the end, but never did. Clearly, the lieutenant did not want to be on testifiable record as saying what he meant, so he just said things like, "You know what you need to do." In response, one shows one's depth of experience and knowledge of how things work by nodding meaningfully. Answering, "No," betrays the neophyte, dissolves the commander's faith in one's abilities, and places that commander in the awkward position of having to say it. He continued not to listen in order to pick up a hint of what he was supposed to understand. He realized, as he tried to sort it out, he didn't even know these girls' names.

"No, I mean do something for her afterwards."

The third one, the one who seemed to have a disdainful, superior attitude toward this whole business, said with judgmental detachment, "You're going to let it happen then, aren't you?"

Scared: "You're not going to—I mean, we're not going to—no, we're not going to—I mean, we're not going to just, you know, let her, uh, let her die, are we?"

Worshipful: "'Let her'? What do you mean, 'Let her'?"

Disdainful: "You want her to—"

Scared: "No, she doesn't."

Worshipful: "Not that I 'want' her to. It's just—"

Disdainful: "So you can have your tragic heroine."

Worshipful: "No, not that I—"

Disdainful: "What?"

Worshipful: "Not that I *want* a—"

Disdainful: "What?"

Worshipful: "Tragedy is sacred. It's the will of the gods. We can't change it."

Disdainful: "We aren't Greeks."

Worshipful: "'God,' then."

Scared: "We're not. She's right. We can change it. Like Abraham arguing with God about the people of Sodom."

Disdainful: "Didn't work, though, did it?"

Worshipful: "'God,' OK? He swore an oath, a sacred oath. There's nothing we can do about it. Look, I mean, like, we're just girls, anyway."

Scared: "But you said—"

Worshipful: "I said, 'afterwards.' We'll all live on in our children and in their children's children. But we can make her into a memory."

Disdainful: "That's all any of us—"

Worshipful: "No, Next year I'll—if you want to help, great—I'll organize the maidens of the tribe to mourn—"

Scared: "But you don't know. The story isn't over yet."

Worshipful: "We'll return to this hill each year to mourn her virginity. When I marry, someone else will take it up, and she will be remembered long beyond the time when our descendants have forgotten us."

Disdainful: "A ritual, a cult."

Worshipful: "I wouldn't use that word. It's a remembrance. We'll tell her story, and we'll honor her memory."

The disdainful one, mockingly: "'Oh, she's so tragic!'"

Worshipful: "Make fun if you want, but girls need rituals, too." She laid out the logic of the cult of Jephthah's daughter. "Tragedy," she argued, "it, like, um, sort of gives life meaning, or whatever." One cannot say, "I have peered into the depth of wisdom and, there, within the hardest diamond in that blackness, found the glint of brightness that shall redeem us all. It has cost me much. Half my soul's been shattered. But here, I bring it to you. Take it now, and know your world anew." Who talks like that? She'd be removing herself from the tight community of teenagers, guiltily professing a knowledge that shames the others' ignorance. It is not to be permitted. And so, to protect her status, she had to make her statement tentative. I paraphrase:

In their hero, the girls would see a figure of themselves. Beset by the patriarchal order—an order that, like the gods, might choose to bless them or might choose to kill them for inscrutable reasons of its own—they could see in her a model of tragic dignity. In a social order they did not choose and could not control, one they were not yet in a position to influence even indirectly, they could look to the sacrificial victim as a source of emotional strength. In their rites, they could make her spirit live, an indomitable sign that the patriarchy cannot crush the girls' own spirits. The rites would give meaning to a young girl's life—not just a preparation for the supposedly more meaningful days of childbearing, the female mission of ensuring the persistence of family, tribe, and nation. No, there is an independent dignity, guaranteed by the tragic story of Jephthah's daughter, in this stage of life as well. "Or, uh, something like that."

Disdainful: "Not going to happen that way. I tell you what it's going to mean. You want to honor the virgin sacrifice, right?"

Scared: "You're talking like she's dead already, both of you."

The disdainful toward the scared: "I'm getting her to see the implications of what she's talking about." Turn. "They'll pray to not end up like her. They'll pray to her for husbands and for children like she's some minor pagan fertility goddess. They'll be all, 'I am not worthy to attain your noble state. I only ask for a humble, ordinary life—with a husband who's handsome and sensitive and has got big muscles and lots of cattle and smart, strong, independent, well-behaved, good-looking children. Oh, and slaves to do the housework. That's really all, in my lowly state, that I deserve.' That's as much dignifying myth as you'll get for most of them."

Worshipful: "With repetition, the memorial will take on a meaning of its own. Any repeated act—anything—can become a rite, a reminder of the sacred beyond time." In the passion of the moment, she let slip out her inborn eloquence.

They hadn't, of course, been idly chatting—none of them had—but spinning yarn this whole time. No family, after all, could afford to let a daughter relax in total unemployment. Jephthah had, in fact, lent each family a female slave to fill the gap in the household labor. This last one speaking, the worshipful friend, relieved for a time now from her duties of tending the hearth—sacred office of the maiden daughter in Mediterranean cultures—concentrated instead upon the wool, the yarn, and the spindle (not the big wheel thing you find in antique shops, but a far more ancient weighted dowel they would drop and spin between their legs, twisting the threads her well-practiced young fingers would draw out into yarn). The divine hand touches and upholds all. By His will does this wool exist. I have it by His gift. My own hand now extends the work of His creation. Blessed be the name of the Lord. "But it's hard to remember the sacredness in chores." The yoke that bears the water jugs and sags all female shoulders in that culture does not feel like a blessing. Schlepping water is a woman's duty, not her glory. "Once a year, her memory will remind them that their role is priestly too. We too have charge over a precinct of the sacred."

Disdainful: "The Levites would see it as an adolescent female Baal worship, and they would suppress it. No one will even remember her name."

Worshipful: "Maybe. It'll be my mission."

The disdainful friend, proudly now: "I've got a mission, too. I'll be getting married next summer probably. Likely. It'll be time. I hope. Anyway, there's my meaning. I'll please my husband, and I'll give him children. I resent your diminishing it, and it's an insult to your own mother. Your whole line of mothers."

Ice.

Scared: "She didn't mean—"

Worshipful: "Of course not."

Scared: "Just suggesting that another kind of life has some dignity doesn't diminish—"

Disdainful: "You sure about that? Yes, it does. If every state of life can have its independent dignity, then none means any more than any other, and it doesn't matter where you stand. Well, I don't buy that, and I think it does matter. If you're not a wife and mother, you're a girl, old maid, or whore—nobody."

Scared: "But—"

Disdainful: "Nobody. You think it doesn't work that way? Then what alternative millennium are you talking about? I'll take my married status gladly. I'll enjoy it. And you won't convince me that it matters as little as anything else. If our friend there has a tragedy, it's that she'll never get to fulfill that female destiny. I will."

Pause.

Breaking the tension, the worshipful friend: "Is it that boy from—?"

Scared: "I think I know who you mean."

Disdainful, giddy: "Maybe."

Scared: "He's cute."

Worshipful, sighing: "Yeah."

And the three of them giggled.

Not eager to press the argument any farther, the disdainful friend held back the rest. You can have your personal tragic dignity if you want to, of course. But it ends when you do. I will survive in something larger than myself. And she thought of that farm boy's thick hair and muscular arms. And her imagination climbed his thighs....

Disdainful: "Aren't you curious about sex, too?"

Worshipful: "Martha!"

And the scared one squealed embarrassed laughter.

Laughter drew Jephthah's daughter back toward them. Her return embarrassed them. She might never know the mystery. They would.

Another day.

The scared friend told her, "Run away." They were alone, only the guard there, not very close, still intensely not hearing. This may now be what he was supposed to understand. The other two were fixing food. "You don't need to listen to Shoshanna. You don't need to be anybody's tragic heroine. Save yourself. Please. For me." If such a curse could land on Jephthah's daughter, it could land on anybody. And that scared her. It made no moral sense to her.

"Should I?"

The other two were not really so very far away, and they caught the drift of the conversation. The pan was heated up and ready for the batter. What they couldn't catch in the words, they caught, across the stony hillside, in tone and gesture.

No point in tact, much less in adolescent hesitation. Serving out the simple meal of bread, dried fruit, and cheese, worshipful Shoshanna told the friend she wanted to make famous, "I'm disappointed in you. Face your destiny, and do it with a show of nobility." Her visage and tone exemplified her meaning.

"I'm scared."

An involuntary snort from disdainful Martha, which embarrassed her at first (she didn't mean to shame her friend for lack of bravery), but then she decided, No, I'll stand by it; that is indeed what I mean. And she straightened her neck to look down her nose. "Coward," she did not need to say. "And childbirth scares me, but I'll face it." Older brother's young wife dead with her first, she knew the pain, the screams and grimaces, the clammy paleness, and the absurdity—not even a live heir to show for all that suffering and hope. Practicing matronly dignity: "I'll face it."

Asking the scared friend, "Where would I go?"

"I don't know."

None of them did. A woman alone in the wilderness was, as far as they knew, unprecedented. Witches didn't count: alone for years in a cave or hut, surviving upon pure cunning, in their isolation, they grew gaunt and weird. How they survived, no one knew; they must be in magical league with forbidden powers. Nothing else could explain such unlikely survival. Fear of those powers' wrath protected them in their vulnerability. What could any brigand take but her scrawny bones, anyway? They were ageless; hardship made young witches old and kept aging bodies taut. At the end of one's rope, to turn to her, in desperation, as a final chance of help, supplicant courted her betrayal. (Approached, she might exact a payment—survival on one's own so hard, so near the line of failure, that the least crumb might provide a smallest chance above the ever-greater likelihood of death—meat, cooking oil, a bolt of cloth, nothing much, just something, though the risks the seekers took seemed to them so extravagant that they were always ready to be demanded far, far more. Sometimes, a witch would calculate, it might be something I can do, just listen and provide unorthodox advice such as these poor, scared children wouldn't get in their conventional homes. If someone wants a prophecy, well, sure, I can offer up some comforting babble, carefully qualified into unfalsifiable obscurity, and if they don't like the lack of plainness, "Look, that's what I got from the spirits. I don't control them. I can only ask. You get what you get. Hell, I don't know what it means, either." Or provide a charm they think they need for some adventure, and they will either succeed or else die in the attempt, and I am covered. Or they will fail and survive and curse me—another cup of water to the sea—that I betrayed them out of spite. I'm glad that they approach me seldom, for I can't help them, and someone someday may be violently angry that I haven't. Yet some witches, as solitude bent their minds, believed they did have powers. They were the more deeply feared by everyone, and they were sacred.) We aren't magical, the girls thought, so we can't become witches anyway. They live too far outside of any world we know. The girls had only ever heard of witches, never seen one. They are rare.

Quietly, "Miryam."

"What," said scared Miryam.

"Would you come with me?"

"No!" and she felt both ashamed that she'd blurted that word so quickly and more frightened now than ever.

Disdainful Martha felt pity for poor Miryam. She excused her friend to Jephthah's daughter (who was really, despite their varying reactions and despite her own confusion, queen of them all): "Here, we have protection. We have him." The guard.

"Will you?"

Martha, calmly, "No, I won't. I'll have a family. I'll have children. That's my destiny."

"Shoshanna?"

"No. What good would a companion be? We'd die or be enslaved together."

We would die or be enslaved together.

Another day.

On an especially hot afternoon, Jephthah's daughter's friends napped under a tent awning. But uncertainty stretched the harp of her soul so taut, the notes that sang from it sang ever higher. Any least touch plucked it, and she couldn't sleep. She had to talk, and she talked to the guard on duty.

"Hey."

"Miss." Professional restraint. He had officially not overheard the girls' speculations, earlier that day, about sex, and his erection rubbed against his leather gear.

That Martha-led conversation had driven her nuts. They would know, in the eternity of a year or two, what it felt like to be with a man. She might never.

But here's this man, and they're asleep. I came to mourn my virginity.

Uncomfortable at her silence, "Hot weather today, Miss."

"Yes …, very hot."

Oh, shit. And she's so young. She's my boss's daughter, for god's sake. And she has been, by her father's oath, consecrated unto the Lord.

"You've been working with my dad a long time now, haven't you?"

"On to ten years now, I'd say, Miss."

"How did you …?"

"How'd I get into the outlawing business? That what you're asking, Miss? Well, first of all, I want to let you know I'm right glad to have decent, law-abiding security guard-type work like this I got right here. It's warmer on the inside than the outside, you might say. Or rather a bit *too* hot on the outside sometimes, if you catch my meaning. I've always been a law-abiding, respectful chap at heart, I don't mind telling you, but when those pig-fucking Ammonites (begging your pardon, Miss) raided the old homestead, killed or carried off the family, they somehow missed me. I was just about your age, and what was I to do? Your father, bless him, took me in and taught me how to make a living robbing people." A stream of innocuous chatter, he reasoned, ought to cool her down. Cool us both down. And then he remembered something especially eager one of the girls had said. He didn't catch all the words, but the way her voice went way way up, then suddenly dropped an octave hardened him all over again.

"So he trusts you."

"Yes, Miss."

"To protect me."

"Indeed he does, Miss."

"If I needed your protection—"

"You do need my protection."

"I do."

Pause.

"Are you married?"

"Was. Like your father, a widower. No living children, either."

"I'm sorry."

"Ah, it's past." Grief. That's what could settle his penis.

"And I," she hinted, "am not betrothed to anyone."

"I know."

Run away with me. Be my husband. Rescue me. I'll serve you in devoted gratitude for all my days. All my many days, if only you will carry me away.

"I'm wondering," she said.

"Yes, Miss?"

"About your orders."

"To protect you and your friends there. Dangerous out here for young ladies. But you know that."

"About exactly what were your orders."

A nod and a wink. Them's my orders.

"What exactly? I can't quote you…."

"No, I—"

"No harm shall come to you…." Half a moment. Did that mean …?

"… never?" Hope and fear.

Does my duty toward my master include to banish myself from his service, to elope with his daughter and hide away from him forever, begin with nothing and scrape a living in some new, strange land? Has he provided a fund for me—for us—in some coded way I was supposed to understand? Would reporting back to him—job done well and diligently, child delivered safely home—be my worst possible dereliction? Is desertion my duty and strict completion of my orders a betrayal? But I'd have her. I would. I wouldn't be alone. Back to my days of wandering orphanage, but with adult experience to aid me now. I can build a shelter. I can hunt. I know how to hide. I would have a helpmate. Cast from this rocky, barren garden that has been my home, her father the blazing-sworded guardian should we dare return.

But maybe that's not what he wanted at all. That nod and wink, I got them second hand. If I deprive him of his capacity to fulfill his sacred oath, I bring upon myself a curse. I interfere with the divine. Touching her would zap me, just like touching the Ark of the Covenant. (Looking at her sidelong.) Too much power for mortal hand to endure.

(Looking at her straight on and boldly.) To turn her over to a death. She's just a little girl. It isn't right. Any god who demands such a thing, human decency needs to defy. Moloch. Run away. Our virtue shall be that we live in sin.

"I must seem dangerous, I know." That can't be possible. I'm just a girl. I can't be carrying such power.

"You are," thoughtfully.

"I need a handsome prince to rescue me."

"Your father is the dragon? I'll not slay him."

"And," more boldly than ever now, "you know why princesses want to be rescued?"

"It's not about the dragon?"

"It's all about rewarding the prince." And then she felt a sudden fear at what she'd just said. "I should leave."

"Together?" misunderstanding her. Her father will send reward our way; he'll find some means to support us.

Unseen by them, worshipful Shoshana, awake from her nap, approached. She thought she caught a drift of what they were saying. "Coward."

"Shoshanna! I—"

Dismissively now, "Go if you want to. I don't care." Clearly, she'd lost respect for her tragic heroine.

"No," to show her, "I'll stay." But still unsure.

"Go on back to your friends, Miss. They're awake now. Go on back."

If this man rejects me, I am going to die. And he has (she took the "Go on back" as definitive), so I guess I will.

She had now, as she saw it, two options. The third way, Martha's way, marriage, seemed closed to her (although the guard, cursing nightly his own hesitation, still wondered if he should, some midnight, wake her with a whisper and slip away, leaving the other girls exposed, unguarded—make them the sacrifice). She could flee and accept a fate unknown, likely bad, one that, for all she knew, she might hope not to suffer long. Or she could set dignity at war with fear and, unlike the rest of humanity, know her fate.

That it shall come by my father's strong and loving hand shall be my blessing.

Another day.

Down the hill she strode, holding herself, self-consciously, like a goddess of victory. In the last few days, she let herself listen only to worshipful Shoshanna's flattery, and she became the tragic heroine her friend longed for.

Her two months' mourning now had ended, and she had not run.

A couple days later, she was back at the same hill with her father. The hilltop (not this particular one, but high places in general, though actually, tradition came, in time, to hallow particular ones) was the traditional site of early Hebreo-Canaanite sacrifice. With, later, the building of the Temple, Temple ritual would become the official mode of sacrifice, and the priestly caste would come to consider its rituals superior to the peasant rituals at the hilltop altars. Once their authority was established, the priests would begin to discourage, then denigrate, then suppress, then ban and criminalize, and then, once monotheism had become official dogma, anathematize and condemn these devotions in the high places as a sinful betrayal of the one true Lord. Deep tradition became identified with holdovers from the pagan past and with the aliens who lived around and among them. The demons who inhabited this land before the one true God had given it to the Israelites—demons who called themselves gods and so demanded a godly due of blood and flesh—retreated from the plains and valleys toward the hilltops (their power from beneath the earth the strongest where the earth lay thickest), tempting the credulous and the ignorant upwards toward the summit, towards an illusory transcendence, a desire for the spirit to ascend toward higher realms, toward a truth of which this world is but a drab reflection. They tempted souls up those hilltops promising blessing, prosperity, long life, posterity, and power. They tempted up those hilltops souls yearning upward, but from them only smoke would rise, not spirits. The blazing altar would unlatch a portal to the pit, and rising from it as pus and odor from a popped and fetid boil, the callused, taloned hands of demons would stretch up to snatch those upwards-tending souls and fling them downward into everlasting loss.

No one believed any of that yet. You went uphill to sacrifice because it's closer to the god who would receive it.

Not normally a whiner, she was feeling pretty tense that day, and she observed out loud that, like Isaac, she seemed to be carrying the whole load of wood for the sacrifice. Not the pompous type to say something like, "My dear, I carry a load far heavier," Jephthah simply took his share.

"Wait, maybe I," she said, "should take it." She stopped and set her bundle down a moment. The goat path up the rocky slope was narrow—one goat wide—so when she stopped, she blocked his way, and he certainly didn't feel like clambering over those rocks as white as sunlight or wading through the hip-high grass.

Isaac had carried it the whole way, and he survived. "If I carry the load, if I do my duty, like Isaac, I might be rewarded with a long and prosperous life, don't you think?"

"Magical thinking there, kid, magical thinking," though the idea appealed to him, pulled at his desiring heart like an ox team on a stump that wanted to, but would not, budge. With the hardness of his life since he had lost his father's protection, his spirit had thrust roots so deeply into the real to suck so hard upon the toughest rocks for the smallest crystal of nutriment, the most brackish drip of sweet survival, that those roots could not let go, could not let him rise from the dirt into the air of fancy. He wanted to believe in such magic, but he couldn't. "Can't expect, if we turn the old story into a formula to follow, that it will end the same way. It isn't the same story."

"It's exactly the same story." And she shouldered the whole load to show that it was. "Listen: 'Father, where is the animal for the sacrifice?'"

He stared at her.

"No, now you say, 'The Lord will provide.' Say it."

This was an empty ritual she was making up. He couldn't believe in it.

"Say it. Please."

With as reassuring a tone as he could muster: "'The Lord will provide.'"

"Thank you."

"But there are too many differences."

"Exactly the same story."

Trudging on in silence for a while.

"For instance—"

"Exactly the same story."

"—Isaac had no idea, and you just want us to pretend you have no idea."

"Oh, yeah, thanks a lot for that. Eight weeks of torture thinking about it."

Double bind. "But you asked for that!"

"You didn't have to tell me. Isaac would have asked for two months to torture himself, too."

"Isaac was a sensible young man. He would have run away."

"Loyal son, loyal daughter. Stupid-loyal."

Stopped and blurted out, painful: "Why didn't you run away?"

She wondered before, but now she knew. "Is that why you let me go?"

"Honestly, I don't know. I let you go because you asked."

Not wanting to give way to the tenderness she was suddenly and forcefully aware of: "What, so I could have been a slave or a whore? It's my fault now?"

"I wouldn't want you to be a slave or a prostitute. No. You're talking like you're already dead."

"What, then?"

"I didn't think it all the way through."

That allowed her, with relief, to unproblematically access her rage. "You didn't think it through?" This shamed him. "You didn't think it through?"

"Well, maybe we can think it through right now. You know, as we walk along. Together."

Shouldering her load, "Maybe we don't have to do this at all."

"We do."

"Do we?"

"We do. I promised. I promised it to God. Himself. We have to."

"Yeah? So what were your exact words?"

"Exact words?"

"Your exact words."

"'Exact words'? You don't niggle over a promise like that. You don't lawyer your way out of this one. You don't game it. You just fulfill it."

"You don't even know what you said, and you're holding yourself to it."

"Look, I don't want to do this. I didn't choose you. God, the Lord Himself chose you. He held back all my animals and let you dance out the door to greet me."

(There was no ram. I made up that hopeful bit because the tragedy was so hard to bear. But I have to be true to the story. The rest now is as it appears in the Book of Judges. There was no ram.)

"Maybe He misunderstood."

"And all-knowing god can't misunderstand. That's what all-knowing means. He even knows what I meant, and even I don't know what I meant. He knows it better than I do."

"OK, maybe you misunderstood."

Maybe I did. "I don't think so. It was pretty clear." The image of her dancing. Ever more beautiful in each return of the memory. Ever more precise in her movements. Ever more graceful. "I remember it clearly."

"No, I mean, He wouldn't demand a human sacrifice. Our God doesn't work like that."

Hah, he thinks, tell that to Abraham.

"I mean, isn't that the point of the Abraham and Isaac story, anyway, to show the Moloch-worshipers they don't need to sacrifice children to this god? So wouldn't you rather follow this one who doesn't demand such things?"

"I made a promise. Duty and obedience: that's what the story is about. I made a promise."

A long pause in the conversation while they negotiated a steep part. He overruled her protest and helped her with the wood bundle through this passage. They stopped for a moment to drink from his leather bottle, catch their breath, look back at the craggy hills stretching off behind them toward the great sea they'd heard of but had never ventured far enough beyond their own hill country ever to see, and then continued.

"What would happen," she asked, "if you broke it?"

"I am," the old thief insisted, "a man of honor."

"But—"

"If I once renege, then who would ever trust me? And then how would I live in this world?"

"This is a god, not some man you're trading jugs of oil with. What are you afraid of, a curse?"

He narrowed his warrior eyes at her. Ahead of him, she didn't see, but she heard quiet anger in the evenness of his tread. "Don't talk to me about fear. A curse. OK, if you like, a curse."

Struggling to say it boldly, but she couldn't, "Worse than losing your child?"

What curse could exceed that?

"A wise commander sends his greatest warrior on the most horrible mission. It is an honor to be asked."

Could I just bolt now? He would catch me. Would he catch me? He could catch me. Honor. Or thank me, even if he never said it, for letting him out of this. Either way.

She just kept on walking.

"But how do you know? Really, how do you know?"

"What do you mean?"

"This isn't something He *told* you to—"

"Well, not—"

"I mean, no voice, no angel."

"No voice, no messenger."

"You made it all up yourself."

Stunned, "What do you mean, I made it up? That doesn't make any sense. Why would I do that? How could I make that up?"

Superior over her father's confusion, "I mean, it was you who decided you have to do this."

"I wish I didn't, but I have to do this. I really wish I didn't have to."

She took three more steps before she said, "Maybe you don't have to."

He kept treading as evenly as the unsteady slope would allow him. "What do you mean?"

"Look, you got no sign."

"OK, for the sake of argument, I'll go along with that, no—"

"So it's like a ... it's like a contract—you know?—and you don't actually have the other party's signature. You don't actually know that, yes, the other party really does want you to do it. You never heard from His end."

Silence.

"So it's just your idea."

"Hah."

"Something you think you need to do. You made it, and you can unmake it."

"I can unmake it."

"Sure! It's human-made, this obligation you've set yourself. There's no, um, like, metaphysical necessity? Like there's no god telling you to do this. You can either do it or not."

"I hear what you're saying, but you don't tempt a god to give you a sign."

"I—"

"You just don't." Ending that line of argument.

"What I've been thinking," he said after a while, "is that the god of Abraham would not—"

"Exactly what I've been telling you!"

"—wouldn't actually want or need such a sacrifice. But he still might demand it."

"I don't follow you."

"Like with Abraham. He acted with perfect faithfulness and perfect despair, and at the very last moment, an angel stopped his arm. And...."

"And?"

"And if ... and if I, if we acted with that same perfect faithfulness, that same certainty that nothing would stop...."

"... the knife?"

"... the knife, then—"

Exasperated with him, "Dad, now you're telling me it is exactly the same story after all. But you never had a conversation with your god, and that god never promised any great nation of descendants for you. And you know, Abraham was an upright man."

That last part cut, and he replied, "And Isaac was a son."

"And Isaac was promised to him. I wasn't." As she saw it now, Isaac had been a means through which a divine purpose might be accomplished. Isaac himself was but a medium, an articulation point through which divine will met human history; he did not, in himself, matter. No promise and no means: in myself, I matter. Was this a birth, at precisely the least opportune moment, of feminist consciousness?

"Isaac," he said, thinking along similar lines, "was owed to God because he was God's instrument. God could give him or take him. Your life had no prophecy attached to it. Whatever meaning yours has is the meaning we make of it."

"That's—"

"Your conception was not miraculous, but perfectly natural and predictable the way your mother and I made you."

"And that's a reason to assume your oath doesn't have any meaning other than what you make of it either."

"Maybe that's true. And that's why my word has to mean something."

"You're just afraid of what other people will think."

"That would be cowardly, but you know, it's cowardice like that that makes men do brave things."

"Ooooh, paradox—how very clever, Daddy."

"Come on. I'm being serious."

Now, they arrived at the hilltop.

Before we get to the end of the story, however, let me tell you what really happened.

You didn't really think an old barbarian and outlaw would suddenly become afraid of some god, did you? This guy's career was based on scorning half the thou-shalt-nots—kill and covet his top two specialties of non-observance. He loved his own child, and he would, of course, defend her from any man or god who wished to do her harm. He lived in a world of clannish defensiveness and outward-directed aggression. If his own clan's god had now become a threat, this was no surprise. Danger lurked everywhere, even within one's own circle. See how quickly his brothers had turned against him when they could. It should be no surprise that a god could behave the same way. This was the world as he knew it, and he must organize a stratagem against this newly alien danger.

Cunning and secrecy. Nobody needed to know the plan. She didn't know it. She would tremble for two months while he prepared.

Having undergone for two months a self-invented ritual, the girl she'd been was dead before the coming of the knife. I am not who I was. I am not. Her friends' repeated-unto-the-point-of-ritual declarations of their scorn, terror, and admiration had, via repetition, lost their reality. She could not any longer feel that they referred to her. Who am I that you disdain me? I am nothing. Who am I that you should fear for me? I am nothing. Who am I that you should worship me? I am nothing. Siddhattha Gautama, the Shakyamuni, would, in a few more hundred years, as he sat beneath the bodhi tree, achieve a self-annihilating enlightenment. This was not the same. This was trauma. She'd torn herself an open wound that would not scar and would not heal and wouldn't have to. It would just end.

And on the way up the mountain he didn't tell her because still she didn't need to know. They climbed in silence, not in dialectical conversation. And there at the top there stood, a lamb in hand, her angel of deliverance.

A clasp to the fatherly breast—so tight and long that it would last, a memory of his redeeming love, throughout her womanhood—blessed her with a second life (granted, she would always, ever after, think "from above," from up the mountain), blessed her marriage to her guardian widower (a good man who, knowing loss, would cherish this new wife the more dearly), and blessed them at their tearful parting with a startlingly hefty bag of gold.

He sacrificed in her place the lamb, sang praises to the Lord, with whom he now felt reconciled, and he descended toward the valley atoned, alone, and lonely.

That's what happened. But that's not what the Bible says. Back to that story.

"I must do it. That's all I know. That's all I can know."

"No, it's not." She put down her load of the firewood.

And he put down his. He set down, too, his fire starting materials. And he took his knife from his belt and laid it on a large flat rock. The sky was clear and blue, the wind a minimal puff, the day just cool enough to relieve, when they stopped, the heat of the climb. The hill, unlike some others in the Bible stories, never had a name; the people thereabouts just knew which one their neighbors meant when they would gesture thataway. Even after these events, they never named it, but they knew the story, and they knew the hill. They knew what it meant, and they didn't need to name it—which means, of course, that in the violent churn of history, that memory would be lost.

Abraham, he argued, had to approach the sacrifice of Isaac with perfect despair. Like Abraham, he said, he had to face the act with perfect certainty that he would kill his child and nothing would happen to save her. He had to approach the task without knowledge or expectation of an angel's staying hand.

She understood that she could never now persuade her father and that she must now put her faith instead in God. She asked, if both of them should then approach the sacrifice with a perfect and a simple sincerity, would an angel, therefore, have to save them?

Calmly, with fear she would jinx his own thought by saying it out loud again, "We can't think that."

She knew that he was stronger and quicker and that she could not escape. In his internal scramble for some solid footing on sincerity, he struggled not to want her to run. He tied her limbs so that she couldn't—like roping a calf.

Bound, unable to escape, she now felt free to abandon human self-control, to wriggle and fight ineffectually. She kicked because all this time on the way up the hill she'd wanted to run, and now that she couldn't she could indulge that urge, vent curses on her father once he'd gagged her and she couldn't utter them. In her eyes he saw an animal wildness. Even a sheep, in the moment just before the knife, can look at you as though it would tear your throat. He bound her eyes as well and set her on the rock.

He forbid himself to think of Isaac's long posterity. As he raised his hand, he forbid himself to think of an angel's hand upon his wrist. He forbid himself to think that even the smallest touch of some angelic finger could more than counter all the driving force of his hand, arm, shoulder, and entire torso as it drove the bladepoint down and into her. He forbid himself to think of mercy.

The young men of the tribe of Ephraim, dispatched along the banks of Jordan, know there is no mercy. And we, we sons of Ephraim—we shall not cross that river; no, we shall not cross the river, but perish on its shore.

SAUL
1 SAMUEL 8-31

Saul is the name for our fears of inadequacy and failure. He is our lost chances and unearned victories, our stepping forward without the confidence that anyone will follow, bewilderment when they do, suspicion that they'll learn their mistake soon enough. Saul is the name for our unreadiness and disappointment, the name for the stories we'd rather forget, the stories we hope our peers will not remember. Saul is the sound of the eternal footman's snicker. I want to tell that story.

Given power prematurely and arbitrarily, unsure how to use it, unsure of his capacities and goals—handed a role but no script, he finds he lacks a talent for improvisation. He makes mistakes, and though he learns from them and grows, he sees himself outstripped by one to whom power seems to come as naturally as clear vision. His own clarity arrives in squints—never a perfect sharpness. My sympathies lie with Saul, the man who struggles with his limits, suffers constant reminders of them, fashions himself perforce in a life he would not have chosen, fearing there is no truth to the self he fashions anyway. He experiences that self-fashioning not as some sublime postmodern liberation, free of any foundational debts, but as a stormy unmooring.

1.

For years, Samuel had judged over all Israel, making an annual circuit to Bethel, Gilgal, and Mizpeh, then back home again to Ramah. Look at a map of ancient Israel, and you'll see this was not a terribly wide circuit, twenty miles diameter, maybe less. He was, after all, Prophet, Judge, uncategorizably powerful figure in the history of Israel, a leader of long standing and divine election, with the authority to settle disputes, with the voice of God in his prophecy and the wisdom of God's own law in his decisions. His petitioners owed him a little respect, don't you think? Say an arduous journey if they wished to tap his fund of wisdom and justice? Least you could expect. His little circuit was a concession, a small gesture of reciprocal obligation.

Anyway, he was getting old, so he appointed his sons Joel and Abiah associate judges and set them up in Beersheba. Their court lightened his case load a little, but working so far to the south as they did, only the southernmost settlements of Judah and maybe some people in far southern Dan found it at all convenient. His sons' court was Samuel's concession to age, but like his circuit ride, he designed it to be mainly a gesture. It was unlikely to loosen in the least the grip of his personal authority.

Joel and Abiah, however, chafed at the tight rein and resented their father for not stepping aside to let the younger generation have its day. Given total judicial authority, but limited in their scope to the most obscure desert hicksville, they got bitter and they got cynical. If their father considered their judgment so worthless, well then, they'd find its true market value. They took bribes. They made a mockery of the law, they made a fortune, and they made, via the contrast, their father's reputation for judicial integrity all the stronger. They also made people question Samuel's headstrong commitment to the traditional government of tribal federalism.

The tribal elders, disgusted with Samuel's abuse of his personal authority—foisting his rotten kids upon the nation—proceeded carefully. "Samuel," they said when they finally booked a meeting, "gotta be blunt—no other way to put this—pardon me for saying so, but you're getting old. There, I've said it. Now (whew!), got that out of the way. And not that you haven't been an outstanding judge—I mean truly, truly outstanding and blessed and everything among judges—but isn't it about time, if you don't mind my saying so, you started thinking of retirement? Maybe some nice little goat farm? Got a place in mind, just beautiful. You'll love it. Look me up next week. I'll show you around."

He knew what they were getting at. Crooked little two-bit politicians, short-sighted ward healers that can't see beyond the next trash pick-up, they approach the Prophet of the one true God with an offer to sell their patrimony, sell away their greatest blessing: the Lord's own perfect governance. And why? Because they have tempted and they have corrupted the judgment of two innocent boys, and they will not own to their sin. Muscular roilings, thunderclouds upon his brow. Guy knew how to intimidate the rubes, but this time, no flinch.

"But before you step aside—hey, cards on the table, all right?—need to make some," insinuating pause, meaningful eyebrow lift (think they're so damned subtle), "arrangements. Believe me, I know what it means to have children turn out a disappointment. God knows it's a heartbreaker. What I'm trying to say: your sons do not follow your good example. They step in? You won't believe what I'm hearing from my constituents."

"And?"

"We want a king. All the other nations have one."

They'd brought this up before, and he dismissed them now without repeating the standard arguments he knew they knew already.

But the next day, Samuel made a speech: "So you want a king." One line, and I stop 'em cold. Retire, eh? "Last night, as is my duty, I spoke with the Lord. So God says to me," Samuel said to his people, "He says, 'What am I, chopped liver?' You say you want an institution. We-ell, you know, we all want to stabilize the world. Listen, a monarchy may be an institution, but a king is a man. I know all about kings. Let me tell you about kings. A king will make your sons his stableboys. He will draft them into his armies, and they will reap his harvest, not yours. Your daughters he will remove from their mothers' kitchens to work in his. He'll take a tenth of your seed, your vineyards, and your sheep and give them to his servants." (Gasp! A tenth!) "He'll take your servants, your finest young men, and your donkeys and put them to do *his* work. A king will make you his slaves. And you'll pray, as you chafe under his rule, 'Oh Lord, how awful it is to have a king!' And you know what he'll say? He'll go like this: 'Hum-de-dum-de-dum. I *can't* HEAR you!'"

The consensus among the people, however, was that Samuel was just lobbying for his slimeball sons. Bizarre as it may seem today, the political theory of their time and place offered monarchy as a solution to the uncertainties and instabilities of informal tribal government, which depended, in times of crisis, on the intermittent surfacing of charismatic leaders such as Samson, Jephthah, Gideon, and Deborah. The people wanted a system that would predictably supply them a military leader and an impartial judge. Is that too much to ask? And they wanted to freeze out you know who and his rotten brother.

Samuel sensed that this agitation wasn't going to end, but he comforted himself that, after all, the people were rejecting God's leadership (precedent for that), not (unforgivably) his own. Wearily, "I'll see what I can do."

Time passed. The scandal of his sons' corruption worsened so that Samuel couldn't just let it slide any more. They had started drawing aside sisters, wives, and daughters of litigants and asking them if they would be interested in doing something that might, um, help the family's case. And now people were inventing suits to bring before them—total fabrications, phony liens on herds or, as in one flagrantly groundless suit, without even a pretense of historical validity, a claim that a whole town—with all its surrounding fields and pastures and all that grazed or grew thereon—belonged to one family's patrimony. Dozens of families were nearly dispossessed because one shyster ruthlessly grasped and pressed the logic of judicial corruption. He failed only because Joel and Abiah understood that logic even better, extorting from the villagers a greater share of their property than the shyster had promised in bribes. And after that, the boys, in fact, began negotiating with that same shyster, asking him to file a similar lien on another village. They'd split the extortion with him. Though Samuel didn't know about that deal, he fully expected their corruption to deepen till some righteous citizen slit their throats. Self-styled prophets were already milling around Beersheba. Bad P.R. to have the sons of the true Prophet denounced that way.

Samuel still didn't like the idea of a king. Loose federalism with himself in charge suited him just fine. But while his own personal authority lasted, he might remain the power behind the throne. Yeah. Stick a crown on the head of a pliable front man, and nothing changes. The Lord, he decided, will bring me a king I can work with.

Tomorrow, a major sacrifice already scheduled, a propitious occasion. I will choose a king. The Lord will show me who. So the next day, he had thirty prominent citizens of Ramah invited to his home. His servants having made the arrangements, he walked out his door toward the sacrifice on the hill, where he would, with his deft butcher's stroke, preside over the killing. He relished the blood-drama of the sacrifice—taking a feisty ram and watching death cloud its eyes, its spirit devolving unto the Lord. The ritual tragedy ahead had him in high spirits.

As he saw a tall young man approach him on the street, his heart sank. So God says to me, Samuel said to himself, He says, here's your chopped liver.

"Excuse me, sir, but could you, um, tell me, uh, where is the seer's house?"

Tall is good. Need to work on voice and diction. The guy slouches. And this other guy, obviously the servant, looks like he knows better than his master where he is and who I am. Good for him: dolt he works for embarrasses him.

"Son," arm around the kid's shoulder now, paternal, "I'm the seer. Come up with me to that high place over there. Stay and eat with me today. Tomorrow, I'll let you go. I want," he whispered with a husky tenderness, "to tell you all that is in my heart."

Too weird. "No, please, listen, I'm just here looking for my lost donkeys, and, uh, you being the seer and all, I thought you might be able to, uh, I don't know, whatever you do, and tell me where they might be. Three days we've been looking."

Samuel, in his head: Kid can't find his own ass.

"Oh! Yeah, an offering. Um." Snapped his fingers.

Nice sense of command. Maybe something to work with after all.

"All we have with us, really," as he sheepishly extended a bit of silver. Looked like a quarter shekel.

Samuel's retinue grinned at the greenhorn, but the prophet himself just dismissed the money with a polite little handwave and an avuncular chuckle to cover his anger.

"Your donkeys? Eh, somebody's found them by now. Come. Relax. Enjoy the sacrifice, and come dine at my home." Drawing him close now so that no one else could hear, lips to the young man's cheek. Hand on his—what's that hand doing? "You, you and your father's house, aren't you the object of desire for all Israel?"

"Me? What are you talking about? Look, I don't know anything about these things. I'm from Benjamin, smallest tribe of all, you know? My family? It's nothing special. I'm nobody." Suspiciously, but too far out of his depth to have any idea what exactly to suspect, "Desire what?"

A paternal all-is-well arm around the kid's shoulder, up to the sacrifice, down to the feast, seat of honor and best piece of meat to the startled youth, gently threatening command that he damn well better stay the night. The citizens of Ramah knew this old politician had something up his sleeve, but they hadn't a clue what. Some obscure plan to save his sons' worthless hides, maybe. They knew they didn't know. And the kid (Saul was his name—Samuel hadn't even bothered to ask, just overheard it as Saul exchanged introductions with some of the other guests), well, he dazed through it without the social imagination to extricate himself.

Before dawn, Samuel came to Saul's bed. Saul startled awake to hear, "Up, and I'll send you away." A threat? An offer? "Come on. Up." Finger to his lips. So he followed, rousing his servant as quickly.

Down the street, the three of them, in silence as the first rays sprung. "Tell your man," who needed no further hint, "to pass on ahead, and you, stand still." He opened his cloak, and Saul felt sick. "I want to show you the word of God."

A vial of oil poured onto Saul's head. And the old man kissed him. And indeed Samuel surged with desire to love. "Isn't it because the Lord has anointed you to be Captain over His inheritance?"

What is he asking me? What is this grease in my hair?

Having anointed now a king, Samuel, his heart breaking, had just tipped sacred history into a new phase. His anger now, however muscular, could never fight it back again to the relative innocence of a minute ago. In heaven above, the cherubim, pink-cheeked and rosy-bottomed, with all the world-destroying innocence of a toddler's anger, brandished flaming swords over them. This young man had to know. As of today, too much rested on his untested shoulders. "Yours is the Kingdom. God will bring to your hand what you need to do, and you need only do it."

What? What is this? What kingdom?

"Off you go." And he left the King puzzling in the road.

2.

Suppose you're walking down the road one day, and an old man, never seen him before, walks up to you, whispers in your ear, offers to buy you dinner, then pours some oily gunk on you head, kisses you, and gushes about how you are just the absolute king. Imagine that for a minute, then ask yourself just how regal you would feel. Imagine you found out the old guy was Chief Justice of the Supreme Court of the United States. Would that make you feel any better about it? Would you go home, clap a crown on your head (kids' dress-up box? maybe cardboard from Burger King?), and start ordering your family about like peons, or would you clam up and feel dirty as the oil dripped down your neck? You'd want a shower, but if showers hadn't been invented yet, you might just slink off into privacy. And if privacy had not yet been invented, you might just retreat into your own mind, letting the memory burble and corrupt while you maintain your outward demeanor. Inward and outward diverge from that point on. Your personality cracks in two as the only way to handle the dilemma, but behold the honor conferred upon you: you have become, millennia before your time, the first modern man.

When Saul and his tight-lipped servant reached home, his uncle Ner saw him looking a bit strange. Saul dazed into the farm like a memory-blanked actor wandering onto stage in hope of some revivifying cue. "Saul? What happened to you?"

Story story story.

"Samuel? Gosh! Really? Well, what did he have to say?"

"He told us quite plainly that the donkeys were found already." That's it. He didn't mention the kingdom.

Nor did he tell Uncle Ner that, on the journey home—while trying to figure out how the message could be true, what to do if it were, where the fuck it came from if it weren't—his overwrought brain had cracked open like a flower bud and danced on his body like a daisy on its stem. In fact, the whole daisy danced and prophesied, each petal a word of God flung to the wind. He'd felt the whipcrack of glory. Some ecstatic prophets dervished and tambored down the hillside at just that moment, and he felt all the energy, all the marrow-sucking anxiety he'd pent up since the weird meeting with Samuel, shoot like springtime toward his headtop, pop and blossom. He joined the crew of ecstatics blowing down the valley with chant and hallelujah. Hallelujah! He praised God, and as he did so, he spoke God's own words that he never could remember after. His mouth opened, and blessed wisdom commandeered his vocal musculature. The other prophets twirled and hallelululated, and no one listened to God speaking through anyone else. To each his evanescent vision, to each a godly whisper fading and inaudible, to each the very lightest brush of paradise, just enough to drive a strong man crazy.

"So Saul's among the prophets now, eh?"

Who said that? Snap!

Come to, drained and high, humiliation seeping in, Saul watched the Bronze Age Hare Krishnas dance away. Each day, I step into a new hallucination. He slunk home no longer trusting even his own brain now.

"Chosen" does not mean "blessed." The ram selected for the sacrifice is chosen. Listen to the bleat of the lamb it used to be, calling for its long gone mother to come and save it. See the mad, red eyes. Hold the kicking legs. It feels no blessing, and it would break your ribs to free itself from any honor.

Shibboleth

3

Samuel realized, with regret, that he had to make the new state of affairs public. (His sons, young as they were, already had enough to retire on, so he felt no fears for their future, and he sent them word that he would be willing now to accept their resignations, which, with ill grace, they provided their prepotent father by return messenger. They had too few friends now to stand against him.) He decided the announcement would require a ritual in which every Israelite would feel he had a stake. So he called the whole nation (or whatever representatives each family could send) to Mizpeh, where he promised to select for them a king. Since Samuel already knew the result, he could orchestrate every move in advance, and as the people watched him ostentatiously determine the nation's destiny, they would sense, in his every gesture and glance, the Lord's own hand. By the way he handed over his authority, he could, he knew, strengthen it.

Like nearly every other man in Israel, Saul came to the meeting. Everyone wanted to be there for this major turning point in the nation's history. Apart from Samuel's judgeship, political authority was so dispersed that, except for a few bloated egos who considered themselves the obvious choices, no one could see a clear frontrunner for the job. So no tribe, no clan, no family felt excluded from the monarchical lottery. Everybody had a ticket in the tumbler. They just didn't know the game was rigged.

Saul wasn't so sure either. Samuel had anointed him king, but in secret; no witnesses could confirm it. He had received no communication or instruction since then, nothing to confirm any significance in that weird incident on the edge of Ramah. And he sure didn't feel like a king—unless, of course, mental illness is a symptom of royalty. He was just a herdsman. He could barely control his father's livestock. It had to be a mistake. Good thing he'd kept it quiet—look like a fool, otherwise. OK, Samuel said he was going to select a king today. So that means he has not selected any king yet, right? Whatever happened with me was a joke, a mistake. Old man was talking crazy. Now he's going to pick the real king. With that argument, Saul convinced himself that he wasn't king, so he felt safe going to Mizpeh. But even so, he feared Samuel might with a loony consistency, name him after all, so he could not risk the ceremony. Best to stay away so the old man couldn't pick him. Eating his heart out, trembling at the cold uncertainly, he hunkered down among the baggage, over the hill from the meeting place, hoping destiny would ignore the tents and camels and settle on a more worthy figure down upon the field of deliberation.

Samuel began:

> Thus says the Lord God of Israel: "I
> brought up Israel out of Egypt and delivered you

out of the hand of the Egyptians
and out of the hand of all kingdoms
and all oppression, and you
have this day rejected your God, who
himself saved you
out of all your adversities
and all your tribulations, and you
have said to him, 'No,
set a king over us.'"

He glared at them for a nine count. "OK, one from each tribe. Come on down."

Senior elders from each tribe: Samuel looked each in the eye one by one till he was sure each felt the Judge's thunderous disapproval of his hopes. He turned his back and muttered, the word barely audible through the murk of his disgust, "Benjamin." His sneer whipped back over his shoulder and cracked in the face of the Benjamite elder, a man politic enough then to bow with dignified humility. Then the clans—same slow, angry, ambition-withering procedure. Samuel's eyes glowed, and his voice rumbled with a thunderstorm approaching from the far reaches of his enormous soul. The lightning, hurtling toward them from continents away, lit a message in the prophet's eyes: "You should hope to escape the curse of God's election. But no, you are too stupid, aren't you?" "Matri." Families then: "Kish." Tension spiked as all Israel knew their king would now be chosen. And Samuel's mind whirled and slammed with the hurricane that was, he feared, but the earliest zephyr of the real storm he was about to loose upon the generations of Israel. "Saul!" he bellowed at a world that was blearing away on the other side of his tearing eyes.

No one stepped forward. Muttering among the men before him (such disrespect!) sobered him. "Where is Saul?"

His father and brothers shrugged and mumbled. "Don't know. You seem him?"

"I don't know, you?"

"Nope, ya got me."

This moment of highest drama for their family had gone weirdly banal. So much for world historical tragedy.

God tickled Samuel upon the ear.

"The King, your brother," the Judge said, "is crouching behind a suitcase."

So they fetched him. Jerk. Ruining the ceremony like that, ya shithead. What kind of stunt? Make us look like fools up there. But what could they do? All that shit could spatter but could not soil the glow of awe they also felt that Saul, of all people, had now been chosen King over Israel.

The crowd cheered when they saw their new king stride down the hill, head and shoulders above his brothers, the tallest man in Israel. Samuel roused them: "Look at him, the One the Lord has chosen! Is there none like him in all of Israel, or what?"

And Saul, buoyed by the cheers (What was I afraid of? They love me.), smiled triumphantly, lifted his arms to flash a Nixonian V toward his applauding subjects. Then Samuel took the rostrum, and he spoke at some length, laying out a constitution for this new government, which he then wrote down and said he would store in the Ark of the Lord for safekeeping. No deliberation or ratification, just Samuel asserting his prior authority. Moving fast while Saul still had no real sense of command, Samuel laid out the extent and limitations of that power such as he (Samuel) considered appropriate. Saul, entirely new at this monarchy business himself, was glad to have rules laid out for him.

Then Samuel, leading the crowd in another rousing "God save the King!" dismissed the multitude, told everyone to go home and spread the news that Israel now had a king named Saul. And Saul hadn't even addressed his subjects. He had feared he might have to and was glad he hadn't. When the crowd dispersed, he asked his master how he should begin now to set up his new government.

Samuel looked at him. "You're the King. Do whatever you want." And he walked away.

"So what do I do now?" he said to the air.

The air did not answer. And he stood there, eyes to the clouds, imagining his future.

He pictured himself mucking an ermine cape on a manure pile, herding goats with a scepter, or issuing, with gestures of serene dominion, proclamations to the shit-smeared backsides of sheep. He pictured himself in counsel with the elders of the tribes and saw this slack-jawed hayseed, gawky and dumb as a mule among the thoroughbreds, nodding stupidly to wisdom beyond his capacity; he pictured that hayseed grunting ignorantly amid subtle deliberations. He pictured himself a national laughing stock.

But he knew he could tell no one. Before his wife Ahinoam and their children, a deft manliness he'd already mastered; among his neighbors, the competent husbandman, the good fellow—with the years, those bluffs no longer felt impostures. Perhaps his capacities had actually fattened into the billows of those costumes. But tall as he was, he felt himself now trying on a suit made to fit a giant loosely, and he feared losing himself in the unexpected abundance of fabric, yards upon yards of a weave he could never gather up to tighten around himself. Surely he'd trip up, and they'd all know they had to find themselves a real king.

So he just walked home to his father's ranch near Gibeah. A band of young men followed him: a mix of the patriotic, the ambitious, the idealisic carried away by the profundity of the occasion, and those blighted souls ever eager to render unspeakable service to power.

His self-appointed attendants settled into Gibeah, well-wishers and influence peddlers sent gifts, and aside from those changes, Saul pretty much settled back into his old life at his father's ranch.

4.

Trouble brewed on the frontier. Nahash, King of the Ammonites, led his army into Gilead and set camp outside Jabesh. He didn't attack; he didn't threaten; he didn't lay siege; he didn't send a messenger with demands; he just camped his huge army within an easy afternoon stroll of the city and then proceeded to ignore it. So the citizens went about their own business while trying to ignore the hostile army at their gate.

Nothing happened. Nothing kept happening. Nothing happened for so long, with such an astringent intensity of ordinary dailiness—nothing happened so loudly and emphatically and with such a shrill hoot of unrelieved anxiety and predictability unbroken for days, that the city could take it no more. Not that they wanted pillage, rape, and random executions, but they wanted to stop their waking dreams of destruction. Fear of what the Ammonites might do to them obtruded upon every bargain in the marketplace, itched the back of every caring hand, soured every plan with premonitions of futility. Moment to moment, nothing changed from patterns immemorial, but every word and gesture became, all the residents realized, possibly the last one faithful to the social pattern. For a people suddenly obsessed with closure, every ordinary act, freighted now with potential finality as they listened always for the first trumpet blast, became (depending on the temperament of the actor) either symbolic, sacramental, anticlimactic, heroic, or pointless beyond all bearing. Or else it became a focus of a time-obliterating present-mindedness and blocked out all emotions and thoughts. Fetching water, singing, cooking an onion, cleaning out a horse stall, kissing a child, repairing a roof, removing a sandal: above, beyond, and shooting through it all, an eviscerating panic. But imagine also a whole town turned overnight into mystics interpreting all the world through the tasks of the moment:

This meal, in which I eat this bread, becomes the apex of my life.

What does it say about me that I end my days haggling over the price of cheese?

This moment to card this wool is given me by the Lord; by His grace, He anoints my fingers with this lanolin.

I plane this board to a perfect smoothness as I have honed my life to a perfect uprightness.

Practicing my harp even as death snips the strings, I defy my enemies with my love of what makes life good.

Pissing against a wall, back turned to the action—what a way to go.

[Kiss]: I give you all my love.

Or maybe not. Who knew what the Ammonites had in mind? Maybe this moment defines my life, and maybe it's just like any other. In any case, no community can long stand so much introspection. An embassy approached the Ammonite camp, where Nahash greeted them politely in his tent, bade them sit, and then folded his hands.

The elders of the town sat quietly, respectfully waiting for the King to speak first. He didn't. He stared pleasantly at them as though they were a tapestry spread for his approval. They glanced at one another, tapped fingers on their knees, twitched, pleated their robes, watched a fly buzz around them, got uncomfortable and shifted their haunches, blinked, counted the panels in the tent sides, got thirsty, scratched, thought about lunch, muffled yawns, mentally compared this year's wheat harvest (nearly ready to bring in) to last year's, sweated, wished they'd worn lighter clothing, let that tune they couldn't shake invade their thoughts again and just barely caught themselves starting to hum it, fiddled with the ends of their belts, wished they hadn't volunteered to come along, checked the course of the shadows against the tent, stared back, wondered if there'd be any fig cookies left when they got home, pondered, worried, feared, catastrophized, and finally cracked wide open.

"All right! All right! We give up! Jabesh? You got it. We give up. We capitulate."

Sweet little smile. "Good."

"Look. I don't care. Whatever you want. Just tell us what kind of deal. We're your servants. You name it."

"Wonderful. That's delightfully generous of you. I'm flattered indeed that you wish to join my kingdom. How nice!"

Not so bad.

"I'm, I'm pleased to welcome you into my dominion. Very pleased. But I have one favor to ask of you, a condition of your membership, as it were. I ask only," as he drew out a dagger, "the pleasure of thrusting out all your right eyes as a reproach against Israel, the weakling nation that gives in without so much as a threat, much less a fight."

One, fast on his feet while the others gurgled, "Delighted, your Majesty. Most magnanimous of you to spare us. Clearly, the tales of your graciousness are understated. Week from today, whole town'll eagerly line up for their poke.

Take at least that long to organize publicity, crowd control, and all that. Meantime, you understand, we'll send messengers, let everyone know the progressive, peaceful methods you use to expand your realm. Nobody comes to fight (barbarously, I must add, in comparison to your pacific ways), we're yours."

"Fine. One week," and a flip of his fingers to dismiss them.

Meanwhile, back at the ranch, Saul still didn't exactly feel like a king, more like a farmer with a whole lot of guests in his house. Toadies offering to do the chores, gifts arriving every day from strangers (running out of closet space), family getting weird on him (all the attention giving his eldest son Jonathan a big head), everybody wanting something intangible, and still, "No, please, let *me* yoke that ox," was the closest thing to a command he'd given anybody.

One day, he finally convinced everybody to let him out into the field alone to tend his cattle in peace—something nice and familiar. Feeling human again, but dreading all the nameless expectations, he returned to Gibeah at the end of the day, and he heard the women keening.

"Who died?"

And they told him the news from Jabesh.

Suddenly, he understood. For once in his life, he felt filled with a potent anger, a knowledge that he could act upon his rage. A challenge to his kingdom— the threat of loss—instituted his sense of sovereignty. He felt an urge toward ceremonial violence, like smashing the good china to show how mad you are. He had everybody follow him to the barn, where one of the hands was about to unyoke two oxen. With a spear, he ran, plunged a clean jab straight into the heart of one. The barnyard cleared: just Saul, one dead ox, and one terrified, bellowing ox stumbling over the soulless weight collared to it. With extravagant valiance, as well as another long pike, he attacked the rolling mass of cattle flesh. Family, neighbors, and retinue peeked round corners (Jonathan, in his early teens, felt deeply moved by this improvident paternal courage), and when the kicking stopped and Saul brought out the cleavers to begin the butchery, they all returned, awed at the stupid bravery. With each hack, he named a town and said, "You. Make yourself useful. Wrap this up and take it there." So every corner of Israel got a hunk of dead ox.

Bloody all over now, he finally felt like a king. He brandished his cleaver before his newly drafted courtiers, waved it around with his blood-wet hand so that the whole crowd poised to jump if it flew. "You tell them whoever doesn't march behind Saul, whoever doesn't march behind Samuel, his ox gets it, too." All gore-caked and angry—man was he impressive.

Across the nation, hunks of day-old meat arrived, and they all said, "What a leader."

The armies gathered at Bezek, across the Jordan River from Jabesh, into which Saul sent messengers. Relieved, but their day of blindness fast upon them, the elders of Jabesh sent word to the Ammonite camp: "All's ready. Tomorrow, you can do as you like."

Back in Bezek, well before dawn, fully stoked ("Got a real king now! We bad, uh huh! You better believe it!"), commanders of the tribal battalions huddled with their leader. "Um, you four, uh, you go that way. And I want you four to go over around to the right. And the rest of you, uh, straight up the middle. Got it?"

"Got it!"

"All right?"

All together now, "All right!" Clap! Pats on their butts and off to war.

And it was a glorious slaughter. The Ammonites left alive scattered all over the plain to be picked off one by one till the Israelites became too fatigued, in the heat of the day, to kill any more. The work had been so hard, the day so hot, that it had gotten to be just too damn much trouble to hack another helpless straggler to death. Word came down, in magnanimity born of victory and exhaustion, to let them go—they're beat.

5.

Saul had saved Jabesh. General rejoicing and praise of the man who had turned out, despite the skepticism of some early on, to be the right choice after all. Some of Saul's most enthusiastic new fans came up to Samuel and—not meaning anything personal by it, just proposing it to him as a suitable authority to OK the plan—said, "Who said, 'Saul's king? You've got to be kidding'? Let's haul 'em out and string 'em up. What do you say? Damn traitors." Samuel said nothing, but mentally noted the first symptom of the sickness of monarchy. He might have said in his own defense that he had denounced monarchy as a system, not Saul in particular. But in truth, it wouldn't have occurred to him to mount any defense at all: firstly because these adrenalized louts clearly didn't have him in mind anyway, and secondly because his own authority, substantial as a mountain, conceived of no human threats. This would-be lynch mob? A slide of pebbles down a minor slope.

Saul said, "No! No one else shall be put to death today, and certainly not on my account. Today the Lord has saved us, punishing his enemies, not mine." And today, at the crest of victory, when he finally felt like a leader, was no time to make internal enemies.

Samuel approved. He said to the crowds, "Come. Let us all go to Gilgal," that is, closer to Samuel's home, "and there we will renew the kingdom." The whole Israelite army marched off, cheering, toward their week-long victory party.

Amid the sacrifices and hoopla that followed, his people happily at peace, his mind drifting toward mortality, Samuel, smug old politico that he was, out of habit, made a speech. "My friends," he began, this virtuoso of condescension, "as you can see, I have listened to you in all things and have, therefore, made a king over you. Now that king walks before you, and I am old and gray-headed. My sons now walk among you, and I have walked before you from my childhood to this very day. Here I am. I ask you: witness against me before the Lord and," clapped his big hand on Saul's shoulder, "before his anointed. Tell me: whose ox or ass have I ever taken? Whom have I defrauded? From whose hand have I received any bribe to blind my eyes? Tell me. Please. And I will restore it to you."

Murmurs assenting to Samuel's righteousness.

"The Lord is witness, his anointed is witness, and you are witness that you have found nothing in my hand." Assent. Supremely confident, he trusted to Almighty God he'd eventually find a direction for this speech. Exodus is always a fruitful topic—use it to explain practically anything. "Moses and Aaron. Who advanced them to leadership? That's right. The Lord Himself." OK, I'm getting nowhere. Fill a moment. "Now, therefore, stand still a moment that I may explain to you the righteous acts of the Lord which he did for you and for your fathers." Um. "When Jacob came into Egypt…," no, wrong tack. "When your fathers cried out to the Lord, then he sent them Moses and Aaron," already said that, "to lead them out of Egypt and made them dwell in this place. But when they forgot him, he sold them out to Hazor, the Philistines, and Moab." OK, know where I'm heading now. "And they cried out to him for forgiveness, saying, 'We have sinned, forsaking you for foreign gods the likes of Baalim and Ashtaroth, but please, now, save us from our enemies, and we will serve you. We promise.' And so he sent you leaders and judges like Gideon, Jephthah, and me to deliver you from the hands of your enemies that you may live safely. He's always provided for you. See what I'm saying?"

No. Got to bop these dimwits over the head with your point.

"But you looked across the river and saw Nahash beefing up the Ammonite army, and you said, 'No, a king should rule us.'" Up on the dais, Samuel was gathering force for his big point. Out in the crowd, the bold ones rolled their eyes at Samuel's obtuseness: Hey, Joel and Abiah! In thunder, "The Lord God was your king!

"Now, therefore, behold the king whom *you* have chosen and whom *you* have desired. And look how the Lord indulges your whims. He's actually (get this!) made the guy king over you, just as you wished!" This wasn't helping Saul's confidence. "Nonetheless, if you fear the Lord and serve him, obey his voice," that is, Samuel, "and not rebel against his commandments, and then the Lord will continue to walk before both you and this, uh, king that reigns over you. But if you will not obey his voice, if you rebel against his commandment, then the hand of the Lord shall be against you, as it was against your fathers." I'm not getting through to them. This is too abstract. Got to make it real.

"OK, watch this. It's wheat harvest time, right?"

Immediately, the people saw where this was heading. "No, please!" Nothing focuses the mind like economic disaster.

"I'm going to call on God to bring down thunder and rain to show you your wickedness in asking for a king."

"No, please! We get it! Don't!"

But he did. And it rained on the dry rich ears of grain that the farmers had begun to reap, rained hard and broke the shafts, damped those clean healthy kernels to welcome gray blooms of mold. So much for victory; God's own prophet had called down a famine upon them.

So the elders of the tribes came to Samuel through the downpour, soaked and mourning, and they asked, fear overwhelming their anger that he would so abuse his in with the Lord, "Samuel. All due respect, but you're killing us out there. Swear to God. Our mistake entirely, of course. Hundred percent in the wrong. Top of all our other sins, we ask for a king. What were we thinking? Mea culpa, totally. Just wondering, though, seeing as how we're admitting complete responsibility here, could you possibly maybe see your way clear to asking God, just maybe, not to starve us?"

With a weary paternal smile, Samuel lay a hand upon the head of the nearest old man kneeling, begging at his feet, trembling with fear and anger, yet visibly chastened, even humiliated. The big man rumpled the little man's hair as though he were a little boy forgiven some naughtiness. "Now, now, nothing to fear—other than the anger of the Lord of course. He won't forget you. His own people, after all. And as for me, God forbid that I should ever sin by ceasing for a moment to pray for your wellbeing. But I *will* teach you to be good. Now then, go and serve God well. Think of all the good things he's done for you. But if you will still do wickedly, fffft [snap!] to cinders." The rain stopped, and they understood him to mean, fear now a spark in the dryness.

6.

And so, under the auspices of prophetic disapproval, began Saul's reign. He dismissed his army, retaining two thousand men under his own command in Michmash and another thousand under his son Jonathan (whom one might generously describe now as a young man, less generously as a downy-cheeked boy) back home in Gibeah—the first standing army of Israel, as opposed to the citizen militia in effect from Moses' time.

Unwilling to risk Samuel's disapproval by testing his own authority, Saul did very little in his first year. Other than telling three thousand men they couldn't go home. And setting up a military command system independent of the tribal militias. And, to pay his army, imposing a tax in the name of national defense. And hiring a network of tax collectors to gather those funds, by force if necessary. No, besides establishing all the apparatus of the military state, he was too timid really to accomplish much.

Jonathan, heir apparent and chief lieutenant, to his disappointment, found military command boring. He spent his days approving mess requisitions, negotiating with the town for space to billet troops, and overseeing training exercises. Dull stuff. "Royalty" seemed to mean "Chief Bureaucrat." So after a year of that nonsense, deciding that he would do something useful with his little army, he attacked and destroyed a Philistine garrison at Geba. It felt good.

Rumor spread. Philistines were ticked. Proud of his kid, however, Saul actually blew a trumpet on a hilltop and shouted, "Let the Hebrews hear!" Rumor somehow got it all twisted so everybody heard how Saul had crushed the Philistine garrison. One part they all got right: the Philistines were preparing to retaliate. So Saul called the militia to join his army at Gilgal to prepare for a fight. Samuel sent word he'd be there within a week to offer a big sacrifice and bless the army. With the Philistines gathering at Michmash (Saul having withdrawn his HQ to Gilgal), that was one long, long week.

As the week dragged on and the Philistine threat grew, people left at home in the villages, without the protection of the militias gone to Gilgal, crackled with fear. Even before modern news media, ill news diffused through the villages and camps like tea through water. As the news of the threat stained people's spirits ever darker, it reached a threshold shade, and they fled. They broke away. Now whole families, now individuals, now two three people at a time would suddenly evaporate from village life. When the stress of that week finally snapped your nerves and you broke away yourself, you sometimes found some of the missing there in the cave, crag, thicket, or pit you had skeetered away to to hide yourself. Sometimes, you never knew what happened to anybody else; you just wondered how long you could live in a hollowed out tree all alone and how, before you starved to death, you would ever find out who won the war. Or you lit out for Gilead, across the river, and hoped the Ammonites over there didn't start to get ambitious again while Saul was occupied with the Philistines. Even in the army, fear would creep up on you—a tickling centipede climbing up the cliff-back of your spine, tiny pitons and boot claws biting in your vertebrae higher and higher till it roped a line around your neck and flung you, too, away to hiding. Your king had stirred a hornet's nest, and they were flying right at you.

How had that premonition of disaster taken hold so quickly? Saul's army was dwindling, and Samuel hadn't shown up yet. A whole week passed in waiting, as instructed, for Samuel. Those scouts who had not deserted reported on the rising strength of the Philistines at Michmash, and surely the Philistine scouts reported on the empty tents and deserted drill fields at Gilgal. A week had gone by, and Samuel still had not come. "Damn it, who's in charge anyway?" So God's anointed called for a sacrificial offering. Before the assembly of his loyal subjects, he built an altar, butchered and burnt the sacrifice himself, and with a fervent heart declaimed the ritual to make his kingdom at one with God, to secure divine favor in the coming battle.

And naturally, just as the last burnt offering crisped away, Samuel arrived.

"The fuck you doing?"

"Uh, well, my, um, the army was thinning out, you see. And, uh, you didn't come when you said you would. So, well, you know, the Philistines? Well, you see, they're gathering, um, a really, really big army up there at Michmash? So, uh, I figured, they're going to, like, attack, right? And I hadn't even made any kind of offering, you know? So, um, I did it?"

"Shit for brains. Moron. You think just because I daub you on the forehead, you're entitled to my job? King, prophet, priest, judge: what's the difference—that it? If only," palms to the sky, eyes supplicating heaven, voice trembling sincerity, like he wasn't glad to have an excuse, "you'd listened, kept the commandments, the Lord was going to establish your sorry kingdom forever. But now?" Finger into Saul's chest, "Line ends here." (Jonathan: "Huh? What'd I do?") "Now, me buck-o, maybe the Lord is looking for a man after his own heart, eh? Somebody who can fucking follow orders, because you," poke, "didn't." And off, with a dramatic sweep of his robes, he went to Gibeah, not pausing to give the blessing he'd made it clear Saul did not deserve.

Unwilling to leave things in that politically disastrous state, Saul and Jonathan followed. (Samuel refused to meet with them: when he learned they were following him to Gibeah, he packed up and returned home to Ramah.) It was getting ever easier to organize the army for such a decampment. After all the desertions, which had picked up dramatically after word spread that Samuel had withdrawn his blessing, they counted only six hundred.

The little army, such as it was, holed up in Gibeah and waited for the inevitable Philistine assault. The Philistines had been raiding Hebrew towns without any resistance. Many Hebrew families and communities, recognizing which way the gale-force winds were blowing, even joined the Philistines. You've got to admit that was prudent.

Jonathan, however, was too young so see how hopeless the situation was. He thought he understood, after Samuel's speech at Gilgal, that he'd never inherit rule from his father, but ambition pricked him, even in the face of annihilation.

He decided he'd earn the crown on his own. The lesson of his father slaying the oxen in the barnyard was not lost on him, and so, to make a name for himself (inasmuch as Dad had already swiped "the Hero of Geba"), he set himself on his own mission of utterly stupid bravery. He proposed to his armor bearer, a lad still younger and more starry-eyed than himself, that they sneak up on a Philistine outpost. It should work, he said, because God has no restraints; if He wants to save Israel, one man or an army doesn't matter. The armor bearer, seeing bloom before him not bloody death but an honored place in national history, agreed.

They would travel over the rocks and then down onto the plain before Michmash, where they would discover themselves to the Philistines. Then, Plan A: if the Philistines said, "Hold still right there till we come down," then they'd stand their ground and get slaughtered. Plan B: if they said, "Come on up," then that, Jonathan decided—based on nothing at all—would be the sign that God had delivered the Philistines unto their hands. The armor bearer accepted as prophecy Jonathan's fantasy of destiny.

Over the rocks, onto the plain, Bang! Bang! on his shield: "Philistines! You uncircumcised pig eaters!"

A guard up the hill saw the two kids: "Hey, looks like some Hebrews crawled out of their holes. Come up here, kid. I want to show you something."

They looked at one another all giddy. This is it! Oh boy, oh boy. So they scrambled up the rocks, and Jonathan, all fear and excitement, slashed wildly at the guard. The blow landed home, much to the guard's surprise, and while Jonathan turned toward the next Philistine coming at him, the bearer finished off the wounded man. Frenzy made the two youths unpredictable: stabbing, slashing, and charging with such imprudent ferocity that the defenders of this little outpost fell before they could figure out how to respond. Jonathan and his armor bearer killed—well, nobody knows how many, but by the time anybody wrote it down, many generations later, the story grew to, oh, twenty before they allowed themselves to panic and flee.

Word traveled toward Philistine HQ of a skirmish lost to the Hebrews, and the size grew with each retelling. The chain of command gradually magnified the loss into something large enough 1.) to justify the attention, at each retelling, of the next higher level of command, and 2.) as it reached the higher ranks, to justify continuing the huge Philistine military build-up. By the time the story reached headquarters, the dead were laid out cheek by jowl over a solid half acre. Intelligence reports had clearly underestimated Hebrew strength, and this incident verified widely accepted but hitherto unsubstantiated predictions of an imminent Hebrew threat. Paradoxically, reports of this incident played into the hands of both the paranoid crowd that urged vast expenditures toward military preparedness and, on the other hand, the peacenik conciliation and non-aggression movement. Both parties anticipated massive retaliation should they respond to this provocation, so the policy result was further expenditure accompanied by withdrawal from Michmash.

Dumbly stunned, Saul watched the Philistines retreat. Whatever trick they were pulling, he'd better find out the size of his remaining force he had to work with, so he ordered a head-count. Five hundred ninety-eight: Jonathan and his armor bearer missing. What now? Dithering, he called for the ark of God to ask divine advice. But still, all the way in Gibeah, he could hear the chaos of the Philistine withdrawal. Confused by this unanticipated tactic, frantic over his son's disappearance, he needed action to soothe his churning soul. As the priest Ahiah approached with the appurtenances of the ark, "Ah, hell with it," and he ordered an attack. The prophet of the Lord having cursed his reign, his people having abandoned him, his enemies poised now to crush him, his eldest child reported missing in a war zone, Saul longed for obliteration, and by slamming his feeble army against a strong one, a melon flung hard upon stone, he expected to have his wish. Who am I to rule a nation? Today ends my reign.

So they attacked the frayed rear guard of the Philistine retreat. How did this look? The Philistine infantrymen, with no sense of policy beyond their sergeants' orders, saw themselves moving back while the enemy charged right at them. Well, it looked like a retreat, which rhymes with defeat, and it smelled like a tactical collapse. They ran. The Hebrews who had joined the Philistines wetted their fingers and tested the wind again. It swung round, and they swung with it. Hiders upon Mount Ephraim looked down and saw the battle turn. They joined it. Saul's troops felt themselves unaccountably winning. Confidence mastered fear, and they killed without pity. And to Saul, this unanticipated victory looked like a miracle, a blessing, a clear sign of God's favor after all.

So the next day, he gave an order: As an offering to God, and so that God may bless their revenge upon their enemies the Philistines, a thankful fast until sunset.

Are we seeing here again the anachronistically modern man crack in two? Does the rhetoric of pious gratitude clothe the king's redawning death wish? Perhaps a part of him was thinking, they will hack through my famished guard, and I, too starved as well to properly defend myself, shall fall—fantasizing, with a kick of instinct, a gesture of self-defense, dagger thrusts wounding his deliverers, leaving them in abiding pain while a clean ax blow snuffs him into oblivion. Perhaps, but the conscious man wept in gratitude and offered up his daily bread as the nearest offering to hand.

The infantry grumbled hungrily, but with a taste now for victory, which surely any just god now would grant them in exchange for a day's calories, they all obeyed. So, yup, naturally, marching toward battle that day, they passed through a wood a-buzz with honey bees. As his army of hungry Pooh-Bears marched to war, it seemed to those weary, sugar-craving marchers that combs dripped gold from every tree.

Jonathan, of course, had not heard the order. Just catching up now, he poked his staff into a juicy hive and had himself a gooey breakfast. Happy faces smeared all yellow and sticky, Jonathan and his armor bearer lumbered into a platoon of Israelites. They recognized him. They gasped.

"What?"

Cough. "Um, I guess you need to know. Your father cursed anybody who eats today."

"Why, that's the stupidest thing I ever heard. Middle of a war? You guys look like you're fainting. How the hell you supposed to kill Philistines? I tell you guys, this really opens my eyes. What an idiot."

Well, they did kill Philistines that day after all—chased them all the way from Michmash to Aijalon—but they were near collapsing by dusk. Glassy-eyed wraiths slitting throats, gaunt stares of killers too hungry to feel, arms almost too tired to lift a club and smash ribs: no passion, only the indifferent stab or bludgeon, another heart, brain, lung exposed to killing air, a job to be finished before night should fall, and then we may eat. Minds upon dinner, not the lives snuffed—one, then another on their path toward food. They were only hungry, and that was all.

As sun set and the fast lifted, famished soldiers slaughtered captured livestock on the spot, hacked quick steaks out of their sides and, impatient to tear into a meal, cooked them barely rare, still dripping blood. Decidedly un-kosher.

Saul was disgusted. What kind of discipline was this? Got to teach these men every damn thing. And mindful of Samuel's recent stress on proper fidelity to commandment, he even halted the campaign now to do it. He ordered that everyone bring to an assembly an ox or a sheep. Then he took one of his own and said, "Here, let me show you how to do it." So they had a mass slaughter, sacrifice, and feast—all strictly kosher this time. It was a good meal to make up for the day they'd all missed—or would have been if they hadn't already glutted on that sunset impulse. But it cost everybody an animal—creatures for the most part liberated from Philistine herds, but still, imagine, for the sake of comparison, being commanded to sacrifice your car.

Saul, sated, wiping grease on his lapel, burped and, stuffed as full of confidence as he was with beef (and, OK, a little wine; OK, more than a little wine), said, "What say we go raid the Philistines? Spoil 'em till dawn. Not leave a man of them standing."

"Sure thing, chief," said a priest who happened to be at hand. "But you think this time we ought to check in with the Lord?"

"You're right." Bowed head. Meditative moment. Then, hands spread toward heaven and voice shouting toward the sky, "Oh Lord, shall I go down to the Philistines? Will you place their necks in my hands?"

No answer. Really, what did he expect?

"Lord?"

No answer still.

"Oh Lord? What do you say?"

Holding his arms out, feeling a tad foolish, he started to feel the doubt creep back in. Somehow, somebody's offended God again. That's got to be it. If it ain't one thing, it's another. Me? He put his arms down and gestured the chiefs in close. "Somebody's fucked up, boys, and it's blocking the telegraph. Want to find out who?" And they're thinking, Gee, practically everybody with the blood in the meat. Is the man looking for a scapegoat? Watch your backs. "For," Saul continued, staring each of them ominously in the eye, "as the Lord liveth, which saveth Israel, though it be Jonathan my son, he shall surely die." And they were all thinking, Oh, give me a break! Irony thick as cake frosting. They all knew about the honey incident. They rolled their eyes up into their foreheads and back again. Abraham and Isaac, Jephthah and his daughter: here we go again!

Prolonging this assembly of the whole army meant, of course, placing the Philistine war on indefinite hold. The Israelites would not now press their advantage.

Saul, still dizzy drunk, trusted God to indicate the guilty party. Main question in his mind: is it me? That sacrifice? So on first cast of the lots, to settle that question, he divided the army in two: Jonathan and himself on one side, everyone else on the other. "That seem fair?"

The assembled hosts of Israel, with a thunderous rumble (they knew what was coming): "Yeah, whatever."

And the cast of the lot exonerated those hosts.

Saul: I knew it. Samuel's curse has come home to roost. My oath falls upon my own head.

Jonathan: my idiot father calls time out on the battlefield. Why? So that he can stand in front of the whole nation and show off what a dumb ass he is. Going to get me killed. Serves him right.

The second and final lot fell to Jonathan. Saul looked at him, puzzled and heart-broken. "Tell me what you did."

"During the fast, I tasted honey on the end of my staff. For that, I am ready to die." He played it cool.

"You shall."

Mutters in the crowd. OK, not like we didn't see it coming, but still. The kid who saved us by single-handedly overpowering (How many was it, nine?) twelve Philistines outside Michmash? (The story'd gotten around by now.) Got forbid! Not a single hair on his head!

Nobody planned anything, but those in the back pressed forward to see what was going to happen, shoving those in front right up to the royals. Now, with that advance, it looked like something was developing, so the crowd surged ever harder, and those in front found themselves pushed right between father and son, and Jonathan just got swallowed and spun away by the crowd. Those furthest away assumed their countrymen were effecting a spontaneous rescue of the Hero of Michmash. Word of the rescue quickly spread till it reached those nearest Jonathan, and they decided to join the already mass conspiracy they didn't know they'd started. And away he went.

The people rescued Jonathan, much to his father's relief. What clearer sign of divine will could Saul ask? The lad was pardoned.

7.

His heart no longer in it, Saul left off chasing the Philistines. He went home. They went home. Not that this meant any permanent peace, of course. Over the next few years, Saul skirmished with Moab, Ammon, Edom, Zobah, the Amalekites, and of course, always the Philistines.

Various legal matters began to occupy Saul's attention now as Samuel conceded to the king a few grains of his judicial authority.

The priests lobbied him to start enforcing some of the religious laws more strictly (witchcraft, necromancy, idolatry, infringements upon the priestly franchise generally).

"Won't that just drive it underground," Saul asked, "and make it harder to regulate and tax?"

The priests: "Need to send a message."

"Message," the King considered. "Jury's still out on that stuff, you know. You guys aren't farmers, so you don't realize what it's like. Worry about a crop and, buddy boy, you're going to want to hedge your bets by screwing a pagan temple prostitute."

"Sure it's the reason. Here, my skepticism kicks in."

"No, really, you ever smell them? They never heard of ritual baths."

"Magical thinking there, anyway, boss," said the priests, "exactly the kind of Bronze Age superstition we want the nation to leave behind. Need to become a modern, Iron Age society."

"Iron Age? Who you think we get the iron from?"

"OK, so the Philistine pagans have ironsmiths and we don't. Dozen gods and temple prostitutes, and we don't. Thing is, I think we can uncouple them, no necessary connection. Science, religion: different things altogether. Sack a Philistine town, kidnap a smith, torture him till he tells us the secret."

"Boy," said Saul, "what you guys don't know about interrogation."

"Bet it's all technology, no incantations to little iron gods."

"What if it is, though? Then you guys would want me to forbid it anyway."

"If it is," said the priests, "you shouldn't be using imported products made with labor of illicit spirits the way you do now, anyway. We need a domestic smelting industry. We need loyalty to the one true God. Personally, I think we can have both. What, you think modernization is incompatible with traditional religious values?"

"Well...."

"You're forcing me to be blunt. Samuel against you, you need allies on the religious front. Back us on this one, and we'll back your dynastic claims."

Done deal: no more witches, and "God Save the King" at every ritual sacrifice.

Then, "Why Samuel," as the man himself lorded his way around the curtained doorway and into the room, "what an honor. If I'd known I'd've—"

Waving it off, "Got an assignment for you." He recentered the room around his own wide and commanding body. "A little background first," scoping the meeting: King, Chief Priest, General of the army, high military and religious officials, counselors, tribal elders, guards, and hangers on—bunch of morons. And he launched into a history lesson.

Like we don't know this already, they were all thinking.

Jacob, as you recall, had cheated his brother Esau out of the patrimony from their father Isaac: the blessing passed down from Abraham. Esau eventually forgave his brother, but Esau's grandson Amalek picked up the grudge that his grandfather had set aside. His great-uncle's dishonesty, Amalek felt, had deprived him of destiny. While his cousins were, by virtue of that stolen blessing, destined to found great tribes, he would be but a historical footnote. Who honors the memory of George Washington's second cousin? Knowing well his own measure, an expectation of an unearned posterity of obscurity stuck in his craw. As it happened, he consolidated and expanded the patrimony of Esau, fathered a large family, and became, in the eyes of future generations, the founding patriarch of a small nation. Diligence and potency—his own and his progeny's—earned him an honorable place in somebody's history after all. Not too shabby for a footnote, eh? But he had founded his nation on a principle of resentment, and when the vastly extended family of Israel emigrated from Egypt, the Amalekites, in honor of their distant father's great passion, lay in wait to ambush the usurpers.

The finger-drumming Israelites already knew this tale: boilerplate anti-Amalekite propaganda they'd all grown up on. *They're not just in the way of our expansion, our manifest destiny; to oppose them is a duty handed down to us by force of inheritance.* OK, we know.

The Amalekite's own story does not appear in the Bible or any other records, so we cannot know it, but I suspect it was more simple: no mythologies of ancient grudges and intra-familial feuds. *These newcomers were, hill by hill, edging them out of pastures and farms they considered their own.* As they saw it, they were defending themselves—not attacking, but fighting back. But that's a romanticism. For all I know, maybe they had a toxic little culture.

And now, Samuel had decided, the time had come to settle the old quarrel for good. "For that sin," Samuel said, "of opposing divine will, you are to punish them. God said to me, 'I remember what Amalek did to Israel. Exterminate the brutes. Spare none. Kill every woman, child, suckling babe, and man. Kill their animals.' The old resentments end when no one is alive to feel them." *Bigot.*

Saul gathered an army, called up the militias. He sent word to the Kenites, who lived peacefully among the Amalekites, that he had no quarrel with them; Moses's wife Zipporah had been a Kenite, so the great law-giver himself had established a precedent of peaceful relations with that people. The Kenites moved quietly out, explaining to their Amalekite neighbors, "It's a nomad thing." That evacuation cleared the way not only for an unimpeded genocide of the Amalekites, but also for an uncontested Israelite claim to anything resembling "abandoned property"—a slick move Moses's Kenite father-in-law Jethro, that old horse trader, would have admired.

Once again, to his own astonishment, Saul generaled a glorious victory, slaughtering the always retreating Amalekites (sure, they knew something was up; the Kenite move didn't fool them entirely) from Havilah all the way to the borders of Egypt. They happened to capture alive Agag, the king. By the end of the campaign, of his entire kingdom, all that remained were the prize livestock, whom the professional herdsmen of Israel could not bear to slaughter on the spot. The experienced eye of an Israelite farmer gone a-pillaging would stay his blade-wielding arm in tribute to the genetic sublimity of a perfect ewe. But the family who owned it, the masters of artistic husbandry who had channeled generations of ovine lust toward that unblemished pinnacle, the family cowering in a lean-to by the sheep-cote as if nobody could see them when the Israelite army lumbered by—they, heads pulled back by the hair and neck stretched wide, each one like an animal to be bled, died by the swords and knives that spared their sheep.

As I said, a great victory, for which Saul gave Abner ample credit as Captain of the Hosts. With Agag in humiliated tow, the jubilant army herded the animals toward Gilgal for a huge celebratory sacrifice. Saul couldn't help but feel justified now, for the hand of God had surely directed this triumph—not just a temporary victory over an enemy, a battle another generation would have to fight all over again some other day, but a total genocide. Now there's something to celebrate. Israel need never again fear conflict with cousin Amalek. The old blessing had definitively landed on Jacob's head, and Saul had been God's chosen instrument for the prosecution of sacred history. He welcomed Samuel to the celebration, "God bless you, you ol' sourpuss! I did it! I have performed the commandment of the Lord. Have yourself a big mug of—"

"Yeah? Well, what's," sniff, "with all the cow shit? Miles away I can hear the mooing. What's with all the racket? Can't have a," pulling his hems from the muck, "dignified little sacrifice?" Samuel feared the answer he would receive. This big man, powerful and old, had felt the storm of history break upon him once again last night. It had rained tears. God had shown him how that weepy drizzle would rise to a flood and wash away His newly planted seed. I repent My choice of Saul, who does not follow My commandments. After that, Samuel had not slept. Circles under his eyes, his face still damp with the night's sorrow, Samuel appeared to Saul as an old man made sweaty and exhausted by his short journey from Ramah, his legendary vigor just today, just now, in the full amplitude of the man's years, showing the first signs of departure. Saul, clueless as ever, heard in Samuel's cantankerous complaints a note of greatness in decline, and he pitied this old man who had both blessed and cursed him.

"We brought them from the Amalekites. Our people kept the best of the sheep and cattle to sacrifice to the Lord your God in thanks for the victory. The rest, as He commanded, we destroyed."

Samuel put his arm around the king's shoulder, drew him close and drew him aside so nobody else could hear this next exchange. "Let's go over this again. You were nothing, and God, in His inscrutable wisdom, made you king, no? And then He sent you on a mission. And then He said, 'Go and utterly destroy those sinners the Amalekites.' You with me?"

"Yeah, sure."

"Then why," raising his voice only slightly, so that the king's lieutenants could hear something was up but couldn't tell quite what, "did you not obey? Like a cheap grifter, you pounce on the spoil. Some regal dignity."

Confused, defensive, "I did like I was told. You told me. We've wiped out Amalek, brought their king home a captive, right? We won. I'll admit I didn't see the point of killing their animals, but we did it. Sure, the men took some of the animals. Hey, why not? But only the very best, you know? You can see for yourself—only the best. I mean, look at that ram over there. Really something, isn't he? I mean, if you were God, wouldn't you be flattered to have something that beautiful sacrificed in your honor? Boy, I tell you, I would."

"'Fine cuisine, fit for a deity. Try our charred ram's fat. Mm-mm, smackin' good.' That it? You think God cares? You think he's hungry?"

"Then what's…?"

Great rolling thunder, "Obedience!" Now Abner, Jonathan, and the others on the hilltop could hear Samuel's raised voice. "'Kill me a lamb. Kill me a nation. Wash like this. Don't eat pig. Let your hair curl rings in front of your ears.' Ridiculous! Absurd little quirks of taste like anybody has, you know? He's got his preferences. He likes obedience, and you," grabbing him by the lapel, "like some witch you banned, like those stubborn idolaters you just massacred—you, my friend, have rebelled. You have rejected the word of the Lord, and He," bellowing and spittling into His Majesty's face, the audience of subordinates, straining their ears toward the conversation between the nation's two heads, "rejects you, sir, and He rejects your kingship. You, sir, are fired."

With shaken dignity, "You're right. I have sinned. Gone against God's word and yours. Yes. You know what? I feared the people. So I listened to them instead. No more democracy. I promise." Jonathan heard him blame others—everybody else, in fact, people in general—rather than accept responsibility, and Abner (who had turned out to be a darned good military commander, a real soldier's general) heard him blame the troops; their respect for him slipped. "Forgive me. Come, let's you and I," like it'll buy him something, "go worship together."

But Samuel had heard him admit to rejecting the word of God. He grabbed the King by the back of the neck, pulled him close. Lips grazing ear, hardly a vapor: "Your kingdom is ended." And then a kiss to the fleshy part of the lobe. As Samuel then backed away, he took hold of the skirt of his mantle and ripped it asunder from ankles to chest, displaying his old-man's knees, testicles, paunch, and saggy chest. The nakedness of the prophet shocked all the witnesses. Age and jealousy for the power he'd ceded seemed to have rattled the great man's senses. "God tears it from you and gives it to a neighbor, better man than you. The Strength of Israel does not lie and he does not repent." Himself? Saul?—who is the Strength of Israel? Man's raving. Somebody grab him a blanket.

They saw Saul approach his mentor gently, with pity for the old man's wild assertions of his slipping authority, a good son honoring a father who, betrayed by age, blames his son for the treason. Despite all his faults, what a gentle soul this king could be. No longer pleading, "I have sinned. Sure. But do me this honor, at least in front of the elders, and worship your God with me." Apparently calmed by the calm tone, calmed enough to pity the speaker, the old man complied.

Amid the prayers the two men shared of praise for the Lord in preparation for the sacrifice, the prophet, with regained professional composure, "Still some unfinished business. Bring me Agag."

Haggard wretch. They hadn't fed him or allowed him sleep since capture. He tottered without stumbling. Last of his obliterated kingdom, he saw the broadsword by the prophet's hand. Prodded, he knelt. He said, "Surely the bitterness of death is past." Blank-minded, he waited.

Then Samuel made a speech that passed, like dust through the galactic void, through the mind of this Amalekite, already composed upon nothingness. "In all justice, as your sword has made women childless, so shall your mother become childless, too." Though that reference to family already vanished suggests a mind loosening its grasp, the bone-severing hacks that followed showed off his butcher's grip as strong as ever.

8.

The King and the Prophet, atoned now in the sacrifice of Agag, parted, Saul home to Gibeah and Samuel home to Ramah, where he mourned for Saul, who would now spend a lifetime losing his kingdom. Saul, for his part, saw Samuel, always openly hostile toward the monarchy but now also toward him personally, as a threat. He had him watched.

Word of that encounter on the hill at Gilgal spread, casting doubt upon Saul's legitimacy. On one hand, as a military commander, despite that bungled quasi-victory over the Philistines, he had protected the kingdom. He'd proven himself. On the other, God's blessing withdrawn, would he win again? Is he King by divine right or by merit? In practice, this question of political theory meant, Are my taxes sacred obligation or extortion? Is the wheat crop I offer the army equivalent to the kid I let the priest burn on the altar, both of them prayers for the salvation of Israel and the survival of my family in this world of enemies? Or is the King a thief who demands my goods at swordpoint? Anyone who fell into debt blamed the tax collectors. Subsistence farmers resented a system that shaved them ever closer toward starvation. Tribal elders, satisfied now that Samuel's sons no longer posed a threat, recovered their jealousy for authority descended to them from the patriarchs. The conservative tendency to honor existing authority still reigned, so no one projected rebellion, but as time passed, and Saul's continuing authority seemed more an effect of human inertia than of God's active will, many subjects began to feel free to resent it.

Royal spies reported anything unusual in Samuel's movements—his trip to Bethlehem, for instance, a bit south of his regular circuit. "Eh? I don't know. God says to me, 'I want a sacrifice at Bethlehem. Take a heifer.' Hey, you tell me. 'Go,' He says, so I go." Shrug.

He's going to Bethlehem: that's unusual. He's making a sacrifice: not unusual. And that's about as subtle an intelligence analysis as teenage shepherd boys playing spy could provide. And after those run-ins over who gets to sacrifice what when, Saul felt no confidence in sacred matters. So Samuel's excursion, though it fit no pattern Saul understood, tripped no sirens, but settled into the mental file of holy incomprehensibilities.

The elders of Bethlehem greeted him nervously. They knew their honored guest was on the outs with the King. "Hey, Samuel! Good to see you. Boy, what an honor. Always a pleasure. Take a load off. Get you a drink? No? Well. Hum. So. We, uh, we hear you and Saul aren't exactly on speaking terms these days. Real shame. Gotta tell you, that breaks my heart, tears it right in two. You two seemed to have so much going for you. Ah well, what can you do? Which brings up a question. What're you doing here? This, uh, this a peaceful visit, or what? Don't get me wrong. We love you guys, but (no offense) one of those things—you don't mind my saying so—one of those things you two got to work out on your own. Not for us to get involved in. End up having to choose sides, and I won't do that. So. Samuel, old friend, what can we do for you?"

Get you politicians a new king, one grand enough to merit all the elaborate ass kissing you could ever devise. But he said, "No, no, a peaceful visit. I'm just here for a holy sacrifice unto the Lord God Most High. No big deal. Sanctify yourselves and your sons, and come along. Oh, and Jesse, could I have a word with you beforehand?

Eyebrows cocked all around.

"Um," on the spot, not wanting to tie a noose around his own neck, playing it cool, "sure."

Over at Jesse's ranch, Samuel and his host sat down behind the house, near a plankway that stretched across a gully between house and workshed. Samuel chose a spot just below the raised planks. Cats raced back and forth across the boards, chasing one another, playing, kittening around. Samuel asked to meet his host's sons. Sure, why not—introduce his boys to the great man, give them a leg up in the world maybe. But why only one at a time?

Anyway, first came Eliab, the oldest, who strutted out from behind the shed door curtain, down the walkway toward the house. Noticing his father and the guest on the ground, he turned dramatically, his garments flaring impressively as he did so.

Samuel: Hmm, tall and handsome.

But he felt no, shall we say, gush of longing to make this boy his master. A gesture dismissed him, and the second son, Abinadab, sashayed out from behind the curtain. He'd let his skirts ride up, showing off his strong legs before the visitor, and rolled-up sleeves showed off his arms. He purposely walked past them along the platform before he turned, on the ball of his foot, to present himself to the visitor.

Samuel: Most impressive, most impressive, but no.

Seeing how intensely the old man eyed his boys made Jesse nervous. Shammah, the third son, displayed himself along the catwalk with inspired insouciance, wearing a sophisticated casualness he found suitable for nearly all occasions. His leather shepherd-boy ensemble, accessorized by thong sandals and suede bag, completed a look of youth, ruggedness, and nonchalant spirit, a foundation of perkiness peeking out from behind a sheer cloak of ennui. Rustic, yet fabulous.

Samuel: Sensational, but it leaves me cold.

With increasing reluctance, Jesse had four more sons pass by Samuel, gave him a good hard look at each one. He would hear the old man breathing harder as each strode out and mumble occasionally, "Oh, I wish!" The Prophet rocked on his staff, and his eyes, fixed on the boys, began to look teary and frustrated. He desired something and feared attaining it. Today we call this inhibition. Jesse refused to let himself imagine what the old man wanted; he suppressed a guess.

At the end of the show, panting, eager, afraid, like a little dog who wants to keep playing, "That's it? You got any more?"

"Um," (The Prophet of the Lord and Judge of Israel reveals in his old age a shameful weakness. Lord, what have I done to merit such a curse upon my house? Tell me, and I will atone.) "one more, the youngest, out watching the sheep. Somebody had to."

Eyes widening with longing. "Bring him here. Please. Let me see him."

And when the Prophet saw the naked boy approach from the fields, sunburnt and glistening with sweat, he felt the gush of longing he had wished to feel for Saul, a pulse of joy as when he first had seen his young wife naked.

The worried father saw the transformation of the old man's countenance from anguish into bliss and feared more deeply what his plans were for the boy. He turned away embarrassed when he saw the old man's hands go fumbling in his robes.

"Come here, son. I want to do something to you. It won't hurt. It might even feel pleasant. Here now, what's your name? David? Well, David," opening his robe, plucking out and opening then the vial of oil he'd opened to anoint Saul, he poured upon the young man's head and blessed him with royalty before his startled father and all the brothers.

By a remarkable coincidence, on that very day, Saul had trouble getting out of bed. Yeah, sure, he was king, but—miserable scatter of barbarians the real civilizations wouldn't flick a booger at. And what kind of king? As Samuel said, blessed by the One True God to command a nation, but can't follow a simple set of rules—engineer who can't assemble a swing set. I've never deserved this (the robes, the food, the concubine waking beside him). I can't (the curve of her splendid hip) even get hard. Some warrior.

The kingly luxury of a linen sheet accused each body part of unearned comfort: I slide away where wool should chafe you.

The doubts he'd felt since first he heard the Judge tell him, "Come with me," had kept him awake for hours that night, left him too sleep-deprived to rise that morning, so he just lay there in the daylight while the slave girl rose and left, while other servants came and, unneeded, left. Dismiss his retinue, uncrown himself, herd goats. Yeah, but no goatherd had so soft a bed, drank such good wine. Lose the girls his influential friends provided him? He'd disappointed this one. She'd never say it, but he feared it. What does she think of me? King without a scepter. What do they think of me on the Philistine frontier? All they expect is that I protect them, and I can't. They raid, and we raid, and they steal our cattle, and we burn their homesteads, and they rape our women, and we poison their wells, and it just goes on and on with no bloody end. It's my only job, and I can't protect them. A real king would wipe them out, make Amalekites of them all.

He wanted to sob, but servants might hear, so he didn't. I humiliate myself with girls and lose my wife's affection for it. Samuel speaks to his god, and he despises me. He gave me the kingdom, a blessing on my posterity, and I blew it. I've cost my family both pastoral innocence and the kingdom they would have inherited. The line of princes I should have fathered will shit upon my grave, Jonathan first of all. Nearly killed him, cost him royalty. Hard enough to raise a teenager.

He prayed for another war to die in, knew he could have one any time he liked, but could not rouse himself, could not bear the planning and preparation it would take to face an army toward an enemy strong enough to kill him. God might just curse him with some minor victory that would save his life, but too small to gain the nation much—just leave in all the towns of Israel a greater hoard of widows, orphans, mothers cursing him for murdering their men. Get me a reputation for vanity and wouldn't even get to die. Whole standing army idea was a mistake—just too tempting.

Summoning, by noon, the energy to meet his staff, he handed chairmanship to Abner, and he left the room.

This happened several times, and Abner started to put it on the agenda. Item One: His Majesty calls the meeting to order, then shambles away muttering incoherently. Word went around: an evil spirit had descended on the King.

Abner put another item on the agenda: What shall we do about Saul's depression? The royal cabinet—a bunch of soldiers, priests, prosperous farmers, and tribal elders—none of them nearly so learned as a modern undergrad Psych major in these affairs, shrugged in near unison, "I-uhn-oh."

Problem-solver, Abner wasn't about to let his exasperation show. "OK, let me put it this way. You. What makes you happy?"

"To meditate upon the word of God."

Uh-huh. "You."

"Playing with the kids. Just wish I had the time."

"You."

"Work. I love my job."

"You."

"Good music. Not this latest Assyrian crap. I mean the good old Hebrew tunes. Give me an old psalm any day. Used to play the flute myself when I was a kid. Huh. Haven't touched it in years."

"Music. We can do that. Get the best musicians in the country." Out of it himself, "Who's the best?"

"Asking my opinion? Bethlehem scene's the hottest I know about. Strictly amateur, but you want to hear deft licks on the harp, that's where I'd go."

"Bethlehem."

"Man, I was down there last month, heard these guys jamming at a winepress, kid name of David I think it was comes by with his harp, and he's like, 'Uh, mind if I?' And they're like, 'No prob.' Old guys, big city they'd be the pros, but here, we're talking real roots. I mean real down home roots. Kid settles down, all humble like, and then he just wails. Left them all speechless, just set their pieces in their laps and listened. Then he really picks it up, and they're all yelling, 'Go! Go!' Fingers moving like, uh, like I don't know. Just wails. Good looking kid, too. Man oh man oh man. You just had to be there."

"Had to be there. Well, gentlemen? Good." Nod to an assistant, and on with the meeting.

A soldier arrived next day at Jesse's door—not an unusual thing in Saul's kingdom. Price of security, stability, and greatness, some said. Every household in the nation, at such a visit, held a breath and wondered. But Jesse had a deeper fear. What punishments should we fear for rebellions we have never launched, disloyalties unwilled. The Prophet arrived uninvited and gifted us with ambitions we never courted. That senile old man gestured randomly in his anger at Saul and burned my son's forehead with his accidental blessing. He spilled sacred oil around my house, and David is the wick of a tipping lamp. If the king should see the fire, he'd crush it out.

"His Majesty King Saul desires the pleasure of an audience with your son David."

My fear. Abraham heard this call and complied without doubts. My son shall found a great posterity of kings, but first, I must tie him to an altar, show true willingness to lose it all. As Isaac's heart under the knife, my son under the power of this royal soldier. Compose yourself. Stoic dignity, obedience. Provision the boy for the journey and as though he were to stay in Gibeah; pile the donkey high with bread as Isaac's back was piled with firewood. Take wine to celebrate the sacrifice, a kid as though it were the offering. God's chosen calls unto my own God's chosen one. My other daughters and sons still live to provide me a family of ordinary destiny. Let David go as though to some commonplace disaster. There was no reason to think he was an Isaac to be spared.

His heart broke as he reasoned himself into compliance, and he barked at David's mother to stop the tears that pumped from his own heart and out her eyes. The parents watched the soldier, the donkey, and their boy walk out of sight. They felt they were the ones left burning on the altar, as though their Isaac had walked down the mountainside alone.

The king? He liked the kid. He liked the music. Cheered him up. When the black dog grabbed him by the throat, then that out-of-this-world harping (what a singer, too!) would loosen the grip of those canine jaws, and he could pat it on the head, say, "Nice doggie," and send it scampering on home. By the end of the set, the king would feel himself again. He resumed command of the kingdom.

Jesse, I want to keep your son here with me. He's a wonderful boy. God sends evil spirits to me sometimes, and with his music, David here refreshes me. I'd be lost without him. Many thanks. You can expect ample compensation for the loan of your child. In gratitude, His Royal Majesty, Saul.

9.

Again with the Philistines. They line up on one side of the Elah Valley; we line up on the other. Big decisive battle? No, of course not. One bruiser steps down from their side, full view of everybody, bronze armor head to foot, mean and contemptuous look on his face. One of those guys who gets an ugly haircut and shaves badly on purpose to make himself more masculine, rid of all such feminine matter as good looks. Armor's all dented, but polished to glowing; the sheen makes him larger. Bright valley dims to dark alley. Imagine that sword honed to a switchblade's keenness, the boulders taking on the intimacy of garbage cans, and imagine wondering how you took this wrong turn out of the Judean wilderness into the middle of an urban cliché. The guilty conscience of the suburbs stands in front of you, and your dream-stuck feet can't run. He wants more than your wallet, and the neighborhood will only shut its windows when you scream. You stand on the edge of an army, but you see your personal fate glint on the tip of that spear.

Shouts up, "One on one—our toughest guy [*chest thump*], your toughest guy. Winner take all."

Embarrassed silence on the Israelite side. This guy has a reputation. (Come into my alley; I want to show you something.) Everybody knows about Goliath. Would you want to fight him?

Well, would you? Maybe instead of volunteering, you would want to shoot an arrow from the hilltop, take him out from a distance. Or send a well-aimed spear shaft hurtling down at him with a hill-height's force of gravity. Or two dozen at once so he could never dodge them all. Take out their strongest warrior before the battle and shame his memory on top of that with ridiculous hubris before your common-sense response.

Hah. You, my friend, would never make a good barbarian. The real barbarians would think you were a coward, shaming your whole side with taints of sneakiness and murder. Goliath has challenged your manhood—yours specifically. You throw that spear, he wins. He's the braver man, the one willing to stand out there and risk it. Honor accrues to his side, and now they *deserve* to win. He's the one enshrined in legend even if they lose, and you're the treacherous coward recalled with contempt in that same legend. You do nothing, it's shameful, yes, and everyone sees you did not volunteer, sees that you compared your manhood to this Philistine's, took out the mental calipers to measure your shriveled balls against his billiards, but everyone around you shares the same dishonor. In your heart you feel the burn of cowardice, the lowering of status and esteem before that alpha male down there in the valley, but chroniclers of legends will forget your name. You're cursed with obscurity, a man forgotten. Death will be the end of your name. Obliteration is the best that you can hope for, better than to be remembered in mouths that need to spit away the bitter taste of it after it's been spoken. With all your forgotten comrades, you shall be forgotten, too.

Yet if you volunteered, so much would ride upon your puny shoulders. "Winner take all." Losers lay down arms and serve the victors. Volunteering, knowing you would lose, you'd effectively convey the freedom of all your fellows into the hands of their enemies. Treachery indeed. Everyone would recognize the selfishness of your bid for personal glory at the cost of all your comrades' honor and liberty. For when you lose, as surely you would, the rest of the army would be honor bound to surrender themselves in slavery, leaving their homes and families defenseless, effectively condemning them also to slavers and marauders. And if they reneged upon that deal, as surely they would have to, well, such base and untrustworthy men deserve no better fate, and they would know it. To volunteer is the worst thing you could do.

You look at your buddies, and you see no heroes. You hope they know, and you see them look at you with the same hope. You hope there's no hero somewhere up the line, and you hope there's no fool who only thinks he's one.

The longer they waited, as day after day Goliath returned to the valley to restate his challenge, the more surely they implicitly accepted it and accepted the rebuke. Shaming the memory of Joshua in their silence, they relinquished their right to the land he had conquered.

Abner, as leader of the Israelite army, had to make some delicate calculations. Goliath's performance was demoralizing the men and no doubt firing up the confidence of all of the Philistine side. The man down in the valley grew larger in their imaginations every day. Big to begin with, he sucked up Israelite self-confidence and turned it into muscle bulk and height. His spear grew longer, thicker, and more powerful every time you looked at it. Abner had to maintain both the morale and the discipline of his troops throughout the crisis. The King's presence helped; Saul was there, back in his tent, risking his personal safety along with all the other men. Royal inspections and the occasional informal walkthrough were a big help. Getting His Depressive Majesty out of bed to show himself was the problem.

During the wait, Abner positioned his forces along the ridge over the valley in the strongest possible configuration, and he could see the Philistines doing the same on their side. He ruled out staging an attack. Not only would the Philistines have a considerable advantage in morale, but the high ground as well. His men would make fine targets while they marched down one side of the valley and then up the other. Spearheads would decimate the ones who didn't flee. The other option, of course, was to wait, maintain the high ground on this side of the valley, and hope the testosterone built up enough on the other side to brim over into an attack we could repulse by virtue of position alone.

More dangerously, what if someone volunteered? Some fool in the ranks decides to be a hero. Couldn't stop him and lose face. Letting him fight would implicitly accept Goliath's offer. Idiot loses, we'd have to renege, and when the Philistines come to take us, the men would know they're fighting for a liberty no longer rightfully theirs. At least we'd still have the high ground.

Suppose the volunteer wins. Always a chance. Then what would we do? March down across the valley to take them and leave ourselves wide open? Sit on our thumbs and wait like they're going to march over and give themselves up? Worse than outright defeat. Last thing we need is a hero.

And so, of course, in came David. The royal harper had been sent home to his parents. Saul had said a battlefield is no place for a boy, and besides, he loved the kid and wanted to see that no harm came to him. His three oldest brothers, however—Eliab, Abinadab, and Shammah—were in the army, and their father had sent his youngest in for a visit to bring them some extra food—roasted grain and some bread. Also, hoping to buy his boys some sweet duty, Jesse had David carry a load of cheese as a special gift for their captain. Saul had explicitly sent him home, so this was going to be just a quick in and out.

The troops had already fallen in that morning and marched off to the valley brink for their daily humiliation when David arrived, so he left his goods with the baggage handlers and followed to find his brothers. The boy looked at the rear of the army he approached, warriors arranged with all their weaponry along the ridge crest, and he said to himself, "Mine." Closer, more loudly, "Shammah, Eliab! Hey, Abinadab, how ya doin'?"

"Sh."

"Our toughest guy, your toughest guy. Winner take all."

A long hush.

David's eyebrow?

Abinadab: "See that guy?"

"Yeah?"

"He's come to just, just defy us. That's what."

"So, then...."

"And, and, and they say," and Abner had done nothing to squelch this rumor, "whoever beats him, the King? The King'll make him rich and, and he'll marry the King's daughter, and everything."

"Huh."

"Yeah."

"So who is this guy? Lousy fucking Philistine, not even circumcised, and nobody'll fight him? Nobody? Royal dowry, and nobody's got the nerve? That true?"

Blank-faced nods from some of the other men.

"Nobody? Not a single *man* in the army? Boy, this really opens my eyes. Hah! Incredible."

He went on for a while like this, impugning the manhood of the Israelite military till the insults—which yanked at big brother Eliab harder than his sense of duty could pull him back—tore Eliab from his post by that big jagged rock, and he tromped over with a big alpha-primate see-me-coming-at-you walk to smack little brother across the noggin. "S'a matter with you? The fuck you doing here anyway? Supposed to be watching the sheep, no? We got any left? Hah?" Smack. "No, how you supposed to know. Hah? Wandering off to see a battle like it's *entertainment*. Watch a *man* get killed for fun because little Davey here is bored with shepherding? These men are here protecting your ass, little boy." Smack. Closer to his ear, more quiet, more serious, more scared, "I know why you're here. Go away. It's just pride." Back off, lock eyes. Point made, he was free to glower again and give the baby of the family one last wallop upside the head before lumbering on back to his post.

Saul's spies reported back to him this incident of treasonous talk in the ranks. They did not say who. The King agreed that the mutineer should be arrested.

10.

"David?" Puzzlement distracted him from his mental slump. *Kid always lifts my spirits. Kid himself is trembling.* "David," gentle and fatherly as possible, "son, what are you doing here? This isn't a safe place for a boy. That's why I sent you home. Treason, David? Come now, son, tell me what happened."

Shivering in an ecstasy of fright, shaking shoulders and hands, unable to still his feet, teeth clenched in a skeletal smile, brain rattling in his head, the boy shuddered in the cold wind of fate. *Good kid arrested for the first time in his life, hauled before the King, no less, scared out of his wits, grasping for a way to redeem himself.* "I'll do it! I'll do it! I'll do it!"

Jonathan, the connoisseur of stupid bravery, pricked his ears.

"No one's going to hurt you here, son. No one believes you're a traitor. You don't have to go fight."

David: eyes wide, mouth set, stubborn little chin. *He must have looked so cute.*

"Son, he's been a warrior since he was a boy, since he was your age. Why, I've seen him—ah, never mind." *Always escape. Slaughter my men left and right, laugh at their bloody corpses, curse their widows and children and parents, then charge upon the next corpse-to-be. I've seen it and never prevented it, missed him once with my own spear. Pathetic king who cannot protect his people.*

"What, what, what, you think I can't fight him? I fought a lion once." *Sure you did.* "I fought a bear once." Eyes darting around at the skeptics. "Yeah, I did. He took a lamb, and I went after him, and I, well, I smote him. That's what I did. Then I, I caught him by his beard? And I slew him." *Uh-huh, sure.* "Your servant," nervous bow, "slew a bear and a lion, and this, uh, this uncircumcised Philistine?" Picking up his harp (not only Saul's comfort, but his own as well, an object that soothed him in his times of distress)—picking up his harp, he entered its world, not yet singing, but—so near now to his music, to the rhythmic languages of piety and of epic heroism—speaking now in ever loftier cadences as he touched but did not yet pluck the strings. If there is any transformation in David's character, it is the shift of the performer striding onto stage, leaving back in the wings whoever he was. From this moment, he would later realize, he would live on stage forever. "He will be, I promise you, as one of them—the bear and the lion—seeing as he has defied the armies of the living God. The Lord, He that delivered me out of the paw of the lion and out of the paw of the bear will deliver me out of the hand of this Philistine. He will protect me, and He will deliver His children Israel from out of the hands of their enemies, yea, even deliver those enemies into the hands of His chosen one." A more gracious bow to his king, and his voice, having recovered its confidence, took on a lilt.

My defense is of God,
    who saves the upstanding heart.
God judges the righteous and is angry
    with the wicked every day.
If he turns not away,
    he will whet his blade;
    he has bent his bow already.
He has crafted machines of torture and death;
    he has assigned specific arrows that
    shall end each enemy life.
His enemy is a sinner,
    conceived in mischief, still
    birthing lies.
He's dug himself a pit;
    he's fallen in the ditch he's made.
His schemes shall fall
    in after him upon his head, his own sword
    land upon his nape.

As the song grew harsh, he drew everyone into his righteous anger. The boy's soul shrank to a tight powerful destiny, and the room shrank around him. The kid smacked a wailing chord as he brought it on home.

I will, therefore, praise the Lord
    exactly to the extent he deserves,
    and I'll sing praise
    songs even
    to the name of
    the Lord...

Holding the note, stretching his voice, keeping up a strum on that high string, diminuendo as you think he's losing his breath, nearly gone, everyone on seat edge, will-he-make-it, drawing it out to a golden fineness, still hasn't perceptibly breathed, and then back down from the heavens with a crescendo you wouldn't believe. Just where did that air come from?

Most high!

(An early draft that would, of course, later be revised into Psalm 7.)

As the boy grew in dignity, losing the shakes and regaining the self-possession that made him such a fine performer, the King roused with him. My men stand aside, and a child will save us. Burning with the spirit of the psalm, he commanded, thundered with the joy of his royal power and in mid-command lost hope and regretted, "Go, and," grim acknowledgement that he goes alone, "the Lord be with you." His unbalanced mind tipped and spilled away his musician, spilled him into the dust, irrecoverably as wine uncupped, even the flagon to be shattered now that he might never taste such wine again. He had loved the boy, and "Lord be with you" was his grieving prayer.

Soon after, walking down the hill, into the valley, eyes of two armies glaring down upon him more fiercely than the Middle Eastern sun upon the greenless rocks, David improvised again in another mode.

> Ain't got no armor, ain't got no sword.
> Your armor's just too heavy, don't know how to use no sword.
> All I got's my slingshot and my little pebble hoard.
>
> My brothers on the mountain see me gambling all they've got.
> My family on the mountain see me throw 'way all they've got.
> If they had some guns and bullets, little brother would get shot.
>
> A man should stand his ground, but a boy should save his life.
> Yes, a man should stand his ground, and a boy should save his life.
> I'm going to walk down in that valley and get cut with that man's knife.

You know what happened next. Even without your Bible, you know what happened next. (And this is, let me remind you here, Saul's story, not David's.)

Fuckin' kid? Hah? Pretty boy! What am I? "C'mere, kid, want to show you something." Sword. Bag. Stone. Sling. Whizz! Beaned. Bang! Thud!

And David, having no sword of his own, therefore ran and stood over Goliath, and took his sword, and drew it out of the sheath therof, and slew him, and cut off his head therewith.

I knew I could do it. All along. I always knew I could. After all, it's my destiny.

Naw, son, you got to *achieve* a destiny. Look at old Saul. He ain't achieved his yet.

11.

Tentflap down to darken the bright day. An annoyance of beams through slits, gaps, and seams. Dust made visible, destiny visible of a king who cannot defend his nation. Saul began to envy Agag. No nation clamoring with expectations, no posterity glaring back upon a disappointing heritage, false gods whose demands don't matter, a quick, gleaming blow to the back of the neck before a long, silent rest. Agag my brother, the emptiness behind your eyes the day we met, your serene Buddha emptiness. Cousin Agag, from the deep of the cave where our common fathers disanimate and discompose into our memories, lend me—I pray you, patron saint of realmless kings—a cup of night that I may drink to dissipate my limbs and mind. I would drink your share of nullity till it suffuses my every thought and sinew. Obliteration. No body. No soul.

Trumpets! A cheer! A charge!

There goes my kingdom, charging down the hill. Today, my reign ends while those macho idiots slam their bodies against Philistine iron and chariots. Look at me! I'm a warrior! I'll smash their swords with my ribcage, crack maces with my forehead, lame their horses by diving under their hooves. Idiots. Like anybody remembers individual sacrifice, other than your grieving family.

I will be forgotten and too dead to know I am forgotten. I'll have no monuments from a people too feeble and too little impressed to memorialize me. The successor Samuel promises to displace me with will find only the dust of a kingdom after my mismanagement. He will be the builder and founder. And he closed his eyes, pressed his arm upon them to darken them further, and flung desperate attention on the dance of phosphenes.

Saul had, like most people, an implicit but not deeply examined religious sensibility, but today, he learned something about God. He makes mistakes. He chose me.

The shout, "We won!" flipped the tentflap. "Beat those fuckers! To the ground!" shone white sun into the king's eyes. "Yeee-haw!" battered his head. "C'mon, c'mon, c'mon, let me show you," pulled him up off his soft, comfy mattress and shoved him out toward the cliff edge. "You gotta see!" pointed his eyes down into the valley, somebody swinging a big, dead human head around and around by the long hair and a crown of hardened warriors applauding.

The King: "Who's that?"

Abner calculated a moment and decided to shrug.

The King, who, just emerged into the sunlight, couldn't tell: "Hey, kid, who are you? Who's your family?"

And David, son of Jesse the Bethlehemite, approached unto Saul, the King of Israel. And the King saw who it was had led the multitude of Israel into victory, and his eyes were opened.

"Son of Jesse. David, son of Jesse, at your service, my Lord."

Jonathan had not joined the rout. Standing by his father's tent, fingering the frayed end of a tentrope, which felt to him like hair, he imagined it felt like David's hair—long, coarse, and oiled. He stroked the fibers while he watched the hero speak to the king, and he grew confused. And the blush he felt when David glanced at him and smiled scared him. He felt as when his young wife walked into his tent alone, so he desperately thought of her and looked instead at his father. No, at David. No, into the valley where they had just crushed those filthy, uncircumcised Philistines. Nothing like a military victory to make a man feel grand. But I'm a prince, he reminded himself. I can do whatever I want. And he looked again at David.

Later, here's what Saul saw: the two young men speaking earnestly, apparently coming to some agreement, concluding it with a manly hug, then stepping into Jonathan's tent, the prince in his finery, the shepherd boy nearly naked. Later, Saul's eyes on the flaps the whole time, he saw them exit, David now wearing Jonathan's garment and sword, Jonathan emerging as unclad as David had gone in. The Bible would one day stress the extreme closeness of their friendship.

12.

What to do about this David?

He strums, and I feel good. Sinking into these cushions, little wine buzz, family all around me. (My son Jonathan and my daughter Michal beaming the same smile at the little harpster—I don't want to know about it.) A tray of candied figs. What is this stuff, silk? Comes in from Eastern traders, and I get a suit made from it. Know why? Cause I'm King, and I can. Power and pleasure, ease and contentment.

What to do about this David?

The troops admire him—counts for a lot more in some ways than the larnin' of tactics or even experience. Don't I know it? Hardened butchers cheer when he struts into a room and can't resist a punch in the shoulder of the boy they wish they'd been. They look in his beautiful eyes, and they see empires. They see themselves crushing nations if only he would ask them to. The soldiers are in love. I'll ask him to lead some hundreds, and this boy who sings like a patter of warm rain or, when he wants to, like thunder beyond the mountains, will expand my realm, my glory, and (the candied fig, so sweet my teeth ache, hold it a moment between my jaws, feel springy resistant sugary crust, crush it in a fruity gush) my pleasure.

"David, my son, I'm going to make you an officer, captain over hundreds. You like that idea?"

David: a gracious bow.

Michal and Jonathan: melting sighs.

Some of the guards, hoping to be noticed by the new commander: straighter posture in their armor, chests puffed a little bolder, professional striving to suppress proud smiles.

David's job was to harry the frontier, keep up the pressure between wars, get the Philistines to withdraw an outpost here, a hamlet there, inch the borders seaward, position us for a decisive assault when the time comes.

Guerilla raids. Attack an isolated farmhouse, who would know? Leave the family's heads within morning sight of a Philistine garrison, and then they know they have something to fear. Lead one band of frightened teenagers to sneak up at night on another, then harden their callow hearts and untempered blades with a sudden thrust in cold blood. Each murdering raid was justified, of course, by one the filthy and uncircumcised have run on our homes and villages. If they splash our brothers' brains against a sheepcote, then their barns and pasture fences splash a similar hue. Clip the dead man's foreskin—Gentile no more—and slip it in the pocket for a trophy. Look at this: dry them to a leather, and I can ring a hand of fingers with my victims. Talismans for boys who fear they cannot measure up to the heroes in Judges—outward signs of valor, lacking inward sense of it—fleshy little circles to objectify the boys too like themselves, the boys they weep for when first they touch blade to human skin. Frightened, above all else, of showing fear or pity, some swallowed salt when first they slit a sleeping throat; others yelled a battlecry to alchemize sleeping victims into fighters they could kill in a hand-to-hand adrenaline rush, too high on hormones to feel pity or fear in the him-or-me. With a pocketful of human calamari, they would teach themselves, they hoped, not to see themselves in the polished blades and eyes-wide-open fright.

Raid after victorious raid, David edged Saul's kingdom down toward the plains along the sea. For David and his raiders to pass through one's village on the way to or from a skirmish was an occasion for considerable civic pride. Parades, tribute dinners, speeches, and someone, inevitably, asking the guest of honor if he'd happened to bring along his harp. Somewhere along the way (who knows where, some kid who, in another era, would have made a top Madison Ave. jingle writer, probably not David himself—years later, a loyal Saulide confronted David the rebel chief with that rumor, and David denied he's written the tune, then graciously permitted the rude fellow to go unharmed to spread the word, not coincidentally, of both David's denial and his magnanimity), the girls started singing:

Saul has slain his thousands
And David his tens of thousands.

Darn catchy in the original Hebrew, I'm told.

Saul was not exactly current on pop culture, so it took a while before he ever heard it. Everyone was humming or whistling this melody, and it started lilting through his own head. So one day, when he happened upon his wife sorting laundry:

"We got servants for that."

"I don't mind."

"No, here, I'll call a girl."

"Really."

Head out the door: "Hyah, servant!" Clap, clap!

Nobody came.

"What kind of palace am I running here, anyway?"

"It's not a palace, just a big house."

"A king's home is his castle."

"You think you're in Babylon? This is dinky little Israel. Hills and sheep."

"Still, the Queen should not be soiling her royal hands. What will the people think?"

"You're worried about something. I know you. This is not about underpants."

"Hm....What's that you were humming when I came in? I've been hearing that tune everyplace. It's nice. Maybe I can ask David to play it sometime."

"Oh, you. You're turning morbid again, aren't you?"

"What. I ask a simple question. Really. I like it. Has it got words, or is this an instrumental?"

"[Whistling just to tease him.]"

"Right. That song."

Whistling again, then carrying a basket out the door.

"I said, we have servants for that! I'm a king, god damn it, and my wife doesn't do laundry." Chased, grabbed, and yanked her wrist, spilling soiled linen into the dust. "This makes me look bad."

Wrist abrasion. "Yes, it does."

And the girls were singing down the street as David came marching home again.

Saul has slain his thousands
And David his tens of thousands.

And when Saul heard this, his manner calmed. He loosened his grip upon Ahinoam, patted with affection the spot on her wrist that had borne his anger, even stooped to lift blouses and skirts from the pavement. He smiled at her, sweetly as in the bloom of courtship. All was well, and she had never felt more scared of him. She fled his calmness toward the basins where the slaves would, of course, do all the washing. And she returned to see him smiling calmly at the cloudless sky and listening to the girls singing, next street over and down the block, but so many of them and with such a pulse of joy that all the royal household could hear it. The King could hear it as clearly as a whisper from half a bed away, intimately close, from the head on the pillow adjacent to his own, from a face still damp with the sweat from a vigorous summer evening's fuck, from a mouth still breathing the garlic of a shared meal, still wet with the kisses of a moment past, from a soul that had folded into one's own—a whisper crisply notifying him of her contempt.

You're good, you know that? But this new guy I met—ooh, I never had so fine.

Not contempt exactly? Just as good.

Behind Saul's smile, the jingle echoed throughout the day and through the next day, echoed especially chaotically at next day's dinnertime as the young hero himself attended upon the king. The echo redoubled and overlapped throughout the acoustically deplorable cathedral of Saul's mind. *Saul has slain his thousands*. You bet I have. And you know what? I can add another. In fact, I see one there right now. Yeah, sure, I could use another cup of wine—cool me down and steady my arm. Up spear (he staggered back, grabbing one from the wall), and find your home. "Ungh!" *And David his tens of thousands*, scurrying away like a rat. Look at him. "Hero."

Courtiers ducked, and servants tumbled pitchers. Trays stained pillows, and the women shrieked. OK, some men shrieked, too, and some women kept their heads. One particular young man, spear slicing his shadow, kept his head intact and slipped away till maybe friend Jonathan could tell him to return.

Oh, I have shamed my family and office. Head in hands, rocking on the carpet, no wife or concubine rushing to comfort him in his anguish, all worried that poor David's beautiful skin escape scratchless. No one pities the despair and anger that would make me do such a dreadful thing. Does no one see, your king's in pain? Can't you see how much I would have to be suffering to do such a thing?

Back out of himself: "Is he all right? Tell him to come home. He knows I love him. It'll never happen again. Please, tell him I'm concerned about his safety. Really. I was out of my head there."

David eventually came back, and the same thing happened again, of course, but after the second time, Saul knew he had to do something to stop himself—

couldn't let it happen a third time. How shall I undo the temptation? Saul was beginning to suspect that the Lord's favor, which he had, in a nearly physical way, felt depart him, had lit upon this golden lad. Samuel had never blessed me in all sincerity. The anointment is slippery. The oil can slide right off me and onto another.

Golden Boy is my greatest enemy, greater than the Philistines and Ammonites combined. Shiv my spine when he finds the chance. I can imagine no greater danger to my reign. Bind him close in a way that won't betray distrust. Honor him with chains.

"So Abner, what shall I do about this David? I'm stumped. If he has a bigger following than the King, this is not good."

"Not good."

"I just don't feel like a king anymore."

"You ever did?"

Dagger eyes. "You too?"

"My point is, how you feel doesn't matter. You want the *people* to feel like you are a king."

"They're acting like David's their king."

"They pay him their taxes? No. They like him, but you're worried they like him too much."

"Right."

"You're worried about you, or you're worried about your family?"

"Well...."

"Forget it. You got the blessing, what, three times? You're king. Don't worry about it. Samuel may not like you, but he endorsed you, right?"

"But—"

"Yeah, I know, the Amalekites."

"Everybody heard."

"Three times."

"So I got the religious vote."

"Big constituency. 'God's own anointed one.' Means a lot to that group. My advice? Lot to be learned in politics from modern, progressive theories of parenting. If you can't beat 'em, give 'em a big hug."

"I've heard they've been saying that these days: 'You should spare the rod *and* spoil the child.' I've never understood that one."

"Look to David's long-term interests. Your family's interests." My family, he, the King's cousin, did not say. "Make your family's interests his."

"Michal?"

"She's in love with him already. You know that. I see those googly eyes. And don't tell me, protective daddy, you haven't seen her pour him some extra wine and then help him stagger back to his chamber." Too much. I've made him angry. Step back.

Saul: seen Jonathan do that, too. "That easy? I just hand him my daughter?"

"You want to make it hard, make it hard."

"I want to kill him."

"Uh-huh. May I make—"

"That's it. My comely daughter is a delicately balanced cheese."

"Snap!"

"Exactly."

Didn't work. The two hundred Philistine foreskins Saul demanded as a bride payment arrived in a basket. David already had a pouchful, and his men contributed gladly to their beloved chief's advancement. For the rest, they killed cowherds and farmers, lost a couple comrades in the noble struggle, but their captain lived to mourn them, to total the little rings, and to marry a princess.

13.

Jonathan: "Dad, about our conversation yesterday. Let's take a stroll. I want to talk."

"Sure."

Out the doors and into the fields. Saul had no capital city, only his late father's ranch, now regally appointed. The settlement of bureaucrats and hangers-on scarcely rose to village size, more an ambitious hamlet. Huts and hovels housed the retinue. Tents sufficed as barracks for the royal guard. Had he put on airs and demanded a gilded chariot, he'd have made himself a pretentious joke. Pastures abutted the makeshift palace.

Herdsmen at heart, the royal pair tromped out among the cattle, manuring the royal buckskin, not caring. Silent, they could have begun at any moment by speaking one another's lines—they could predict the whole approaching conversation so well. Saul had, the day before, asked Jonathan to help him kill David.

He'll tell me my request is shameful, conspiring to kill the innocent. He'll never mention their, uh, friendship. Too skilled a rhetorician to remind me of that obvious personal interest of his. Put it all in terms of my own interest.

And through Jonathan's mind: He'll remind me blood is thicker than. To whom my first duty. If I'm to succeed. Rival for the.

Wait. Wait. Wait. OK, OK, right here. Near enough? Yes. And Jonathan took the high road: "Let not the King sin against his servant, against David; because he hath not sinned against thee, and because his works have been to thee-ward very good. For he put his life in his hand and slew the Philistine, and the Lord wrought a great salvation for all Israel; thou sawest it and did rejoice: wherefore then wilt thou sin against innocent blood to slay David without cause?"

Well, when you put it that way....

Indeed, he found he could not follow through with the speech he'd planned to give his son. He felt ashamed. What had David ever done to him? *Worm that I am, I really do not deserve such a good son, such a good servant. What was I thinking?* His eyes moistened, his gaze slid toward the dust, his chin slumped into his chest, and his shoulders drooped, carrying now the moral weight of his proposal that Jonathan murder his friend. "As the Lord liveth," hand on the young man's shoulder, eyes on the dirt by the young man's feet, balding forehead blazing shame before the young man's face, "he shall not be slain. I'm so sorry." And he cried.

Fingers to lips: "WHEEEYOOOWHHIT! Hey! David! It's all right! Come out now!"

"He was behind this rock the whole time?"

"Yeah. Hey, David! Come on. It's OK."

"He heard the whole thing?"

"Yes, I heard the whole thing."

A hard mutual stare through a long moment.

Then, "I'm [sob!] so sorry! I'm a pathetic leader. Really, I am. I'm so sorry." Face thoroughly moist, wiping snot and tears on David's tunic-shoulder, arms around the triumphant shepherd. "Really. Everything—I swear, everything just like before. Oh, my own son-in-law! David, you're a son to me, really. I don't deserve you should ever, ever forgive me. How could I?" Long he clung through a truly cleansing jag of tears.

Honestly, it was pathetic.

As before, David played and sang each day, and Saul's depression lifted. Months passed, and all remained happy in the royal household. More months passed, and Saul couldn't help but notice that Michal continued to keep her girlish figure. And his sweet-tempered daughter would glare, snap, and pine. She was a teenager, sure, so sullen and moody were to be expected. Still, what teeny-bopper wouldn't thrill to marry *the* all-time heartthrob of Jewish history? Could it be that that big dick Michelangelo would one day so lovingly shape and polish simply didn't rev when you cranked the starter? Like most successful men, Saul, in his optimistic and expansive moods, considered himself an expert on nearly everything, including, in this case, adolescent sexual dysfunction. Lately, his own drive had been rolling along just fine, so it felt good, too, to think he saw a fault in wonderboy, some capacity where the old man still held an advantage.

Ahinoam, when asked: "You think a sixteen-year-old talks to her mother about these things? I mean except in utter desperation?"

"You want me to talk to her?"

When she finished laughing: "Oh, go ahead, you, if you think it'll do any good." And she playfully flicked a pillowcase at him, "But I already did."

"And?"

"Oh, talk to her yourself for all the good it'll do."

So later that day, after the meetings and briefings, the reception of dignitaries and the dispatch of ambassadors, reviews of troops and of policies, consultation, legislation, and declaration; after all the business of government that day, business which, by the way, Saul was starting, after several years, to feel he was getting the hang of (the big suit beginning to fit)—at the end of that day, he spoke to his daughter alone.

"Honey," he said, "I know that sometimes young people enter marriage with some, well, very high expectations, and I was wondering if maybe there was something that wasn't working out quite the way you had hoped. I don't mean to pry, but I couldn't help noticing lately that you're, well, not yourself, and—"

"Daddy, I want sex."

Um.

"I want him in any hole he cares to stick it. I want him to rattle my hipbones till they chime. I want him to stretch me wide and snap me like a rubber band. I want to come like a bust dam and sing in high soprano. I want to fuck him till he wobbles."

Not the conversation he'd envisioned. Where did my daughter learn to speak this way?

"Daddy, can't you see?"

"So really, you never?"

"But right *now* he won't."

"But you do."

"What can I say? The guy's a musician. He's got rhythm."

Not hep to that swing jive, Saul let his face blank, hoping for an explanation.

"He doesn't want babies. He doesn't want *my* babies."

Saliva chilled in his mouth. The King swallowed ice and felt vital warmth collapse into the cold center of his belly. So he is my enemy.

14.

He does not want to father rivals, the blood of Saul recovering, a generation hence, the crown he plans to steal—grandsons, magnets to malcontents and rebels.

Or patriots loyal to my memory. My memory. He would make me historical. My sons, too, should watch their backs. Jonathan my son, David has felt around on you for just the spot to slide his blade. This is depressing. I loved that kid. He made me happy. But now I know.

Saul moped. At the time for the evening meal, David gladhanded his way into the room, giving each courtier the exact right attention: a backslap to this one, a confidential whisper to that, a solemn nod, a frisky wink, a touch to the elbow, or just eye contact—everybody's best friend. Chests swelled and faces glowed all around the room as the most charming man in Israel burnished the self-esteem of attendants and dignitaries alike with his stardust personality.

Out of the heavy burden of duty to his family, Saul reached again back toward the spearshafts. I've done this before, and it never works.

And it didn't work this time, either. David rolled away and zipped out the door just a zit's breadth away from the spearhead. Old man's aim's improved. Maybe he means it this time. "Michal, your old man's gone nuts!"

Up from her needlework, "Daddy?" What did I say? I ticked him off. What did I do? He's gone bussalouie. I knew it. "Go. Run away. He'll kill you."

"No shit. The spear?"

"Go! Oooooh!" She grabbed him, mostly with her thighs, and ground her crotch against his middle as she tongued him deep. She rubbed her chest against his own and felt him harden.

"I'm—" he cupped a breast with one hand, bottom with the other as she slammed against him.

The way she squeaked when she was coming, "Just get out of here!" and she nearly bit his lips off as she pushed him out the window.

Onto the first floor roof, scrambled down, and away.

Michal took the household gods (yep, Saul had been hedging his metaphysical bets), laid them in the bed along with a hank of goat hair at the head, and then a, "Sh, he's sick," when the constables arrived.

"Then," every damn thing, "bring him in the bed, and I'll murder him myself."

So back they went, and, "Well, we'll just see for ourselves, then, won't we? Oh. Oh, my. This is going to. Oh, my, what shall we? Do you think? He'll." Dither. "Yes. All right, there, Missy, just you wait till your father hears about *this*." No, a tip for the messenger at the end of that spearshaft. We can't just. "Never you mind about *that* now, thank you very much. You just march your pretty little self right on down there." And he primly marched her down to her father, pleased with himself for having found a way out of that little difficulty.

But his partner, more depressive, more intellectual, more of a radical in his way, saw in his doom yet another instance of the common people crushed in the clashes between factions of the ruling class. I am an ant between the millstones, and so are you, my friend. We are arresting the King's daughter. He will not thank us.

Down the hall and into the royal chamber with her. "[Dry little cough.]"

"Yes?"

"Majesty, the fugitive had an accomplice."

"Fugitive?"

Don't speak. Direct the focus onto her. Gesture her forward into a position where she's the addressee. Good, good. Now fade into the tapestry.

"Fugitive."

And she just stared at him with the biggest, cutest, saddest eyes you could ever imagine. Permit me here to deploy a cliché: the adorable big-eyed waif.

Finally getting it, "Michal! Honey! Daddy's little sweety-pie. Conniving bitch. He's my enemy. You know that, don't you?"

Who could hurt those big wet eyes?

"Why'd you let him escape?"

"'Let him'? 'Let him'? You know what that man is like?" Angrily, at her brother, "You know what he said to his *wife* that he won't sleep with?"

Jonathan: "What? I know for a fact that—"

"What he said to his liegelord's daughter? Huh? Do you?"

Saul: "We're wasting time here. You two, run." [The guards: Whew! We made it.] "Now!" [And they were gone.]

Michal: "'Why shouldn't I kill you? Give me one reason.' And he really wanted to know."

Saul: "So you...."

"Slow him down by the time it takes him to kill me? Is that what you think I should have done?"

"Honey pie."

"Oh, Daddy, you make me so mad sometimes." Stomped her little foot.

15.

Fucker's gonna kill me. Fucker's gonna kill me. Fucker's gonna kill me. Fucker's gonna kill me. Fucker's gonna kill me. Fucker's gonna kill me. Fucker's gonna kill me. Fucker's gonna kill me. Fucker's gonna kill me. Fucker's gonna kill me. Fucker's gonna kill me. Fucker's gonna kill me. Fucker's gonna kill me.

Though Saul may have thought this, it was David, the eloquent young poet, who muttered it as he ran. The rhythm and the motive sped him on. For David faced the same politico-epistemological dilemma as Saul: how can I know I am

King? Old man's whim, secret consecration, open hostility of currently constituted authority, and despite a habitually sparkling self-confidence such as Saul would never know, a suspicion that God either makes mistakes (current doozy on the throne now a case in point) or has no role at all in the political process: two fairly disturbing possibilities for the lad who was supposed to be a man after the Lord's own heart. And like he could trust the old man's word or something, he ran, hid out, ran some more, pilfered, cowered, snuck, and ran still more all the way to Ramah to ask Samuel just what the fuck. He figured he was outrunning any Wanted posters, but still, to be seen would tip off his pursuers. Couldn't let them know he was headed toward Samuel.

Abner: "Probably toward Samuel."

Saul: "Yuh think?"

"Stands to reason. You two." Second guard: Oh shit, oh shit, oh shit, not again. "This time we want him dead."

Fucker's gonna kill me.

Up the hill at Ramah, winded like never before in his life. Fear, bewilderment, doubt. Do we live out our destiny, or do things just happen? "Samuel! Samuel! I need help." Bolting toward the door, "Let me in! Where are y— Oh! Samuel! You must. I'm. Ho. Hah. Whew! Samuel, I."

"And they always come crawling back. 'Give us a ki-ing. Give us a ki-ing.' And look how God mocks them. Sweaty little bag of majesty lands on my front stoop with a lit match and a door chime, and they expect me to soil my slippers. Well, nothing doing, pal. I fell for that before. Always come cr—. I was adjudicating tribal boundaries before you were out of—"

"Right. Right. Samuel—"

"Damn right, I'm right. Who needs the Word of the Lord when you can ask some cow-caked herdboy to direct the national destiny?"

"Samuel, you know I have always had the deepest respect for you and your work. Man, nobody, but nobody, can cut through the intricacies of the law as you can with your learned hand. Greatest judge we've had. You make kings and unmake them. Nations are destroyed at your word. What can I say? I got a problem? I come to you."

A petitioner at his feet again after so long, the years now of progressively more honorless isolation, the crotchety old man felt his joints loosen, felt the dark, cool little room begin to glow. One comes to me with reverence, in need, seeking succor and justice. The Lord's own chosen. He warmed, felt his face brighten, his skin shine unseen beneath his linen garments. He felt each breath now a draught of cool wine. His head lightened, and his eyesight sharpened. His arms felt strong. He had never retired, but the nation had stopped turning to him. The aura of authority, though still might it shine, had received less and less reflection. So the world he lived in had dimmed as occasions diminished for displays of his power. His flame, unseen, would not illuminate; it would not warm him. Yet this boy who brings kindling to my embers is indeed blessed, rekindling in my soul the spirit of the Lord. "All things are possible," gruffness turning tender, "my boy."

"Samuel, he wants my head."

"You come here to duck a spearshaft 'fore my table? You run here to train his arrows on my window? You aim his fury down upon my household? Draw bull's eyes on my walls with your own blood, why don't you?" This wasn't anger. He was amused, really pleased to be back in the center of the political action. "A tactical retreat unto my villa at Naioth would not, I dare say, be altogether unwarranted." Oh! he was enjoying himself.

Of which, before nightfall, spies informed the King.

Who, to his general Abner, "You said Ramah."

"Same diff."

"You sent the guards to Ramah."

"Your Majesty," said the Chief Royal Spy, "I know the men of whom you speak."

"Yeah?"

"Met them on the way. Redirected their path." Poor stiffs.

["*Naioth? You're shitting me.*"

"*My own ears.*"

"*Wait one moment, there, Buster Brown. Ramah. Our orders specifically said Ramah, gosh darn it.*"

"*Our what? 'Kill him.'*"

"*Specifically stated—*"

"*Listen, man, you got to analyze the political context. Struggles between factions of the ruling class may seem at first glance irrelevant to the fates of the lower classes, but the devastation each faction may be willing to meet upon the society as a whole in order to pursue its own interests—*"

"*Now don't you go and confuse me with any of your communistic mumbo-jumbo.*"

"*OK, spy, you tell him.*"

"*Y'ask me? I say I never saw a king his interests weren't served by a nice pro-active murder.*"]

To Naioth.

Where Samuel, his villa surrounded by the babble of the would-be prophets who accumulated around him wherever he went, dilated upon political tactics. "What you want to do, kid, is get yourself a political advisor. Name of the game. Somebody to bounce ideas off of. Now you take your buddy Saul, here. Knows he don't know what the fuck he's doing, making it up as he goes along, bunch of yes-men all around him he doesn't dare ask advice from cause he knows whatever ideas he pisses out, they'll, 'Uh-huh, yup, yup, 'nother good one, Boss.'

"And another thing. Obedience. Know your limits. Crown boy over there? No way. You got your secular, you got your sacred. Know what I'm saying? Line to be drawn."

"So the ethical constraints of one…."

How do you answer that one? Samuel stared across at his nation's destiny. Any king's a curse upon us all, but this one, I can love. He cuts to the heart, sees the distinctions and the paradoxes. "You," leaning forward, his heart aching with joy and sadness, "are a man after the Lord's own heart. His own heart. What you shall lay your hand to, it shall not go amiss. The generations shall sing praises to your name. And your sons and their descent shall rule a nation for ages to come. This," wondering how to convey the full weight of what he was saying here, the blessing and the curse of chosenness, the searing brightness and velvety soft dark horror, "is the Word of the Lord."

16.

Joel and Abbiah re-enter the story.

"'Bout time."

"So what are we, some kind of plot device or something? Bring us in only when you need to kick start an episode? Hey, how about a little respect for a couple of retired judges."

"Any money in being a plot device?"

"What do you think."

Abbiah, leaving: "I'm out of here."

Joel: "Hey, spy!"

"Yeah?"

"Schmuck's gone. Now let's deal."

"What? Your own father? You know what the orders are?"

Cold stare.

"You're not scared of…? Geez, man, don't you know we're living in a patriarchal society? I mean…, and you'd betray even him?"

"You got a problem with that?"

Sigh. "Deep as I am, down I go, still deeper."

"Here's the deal. Meetcha this spot. You bring me the assassins, I bring them the rest of the way."

"For?"

Dicker.

Dicker.

Deal.

Our two brave fighting men, Soldier I and Soldier II, met up with Joel and, with him, approached Samuel's villa at Naioth.

"Broad daylight?"

"What, I should sneak up on my own father's house like a thief?"

"Well I, for one, unlike my colleague here, am not the least teeny bit ashamed to carry out the commands of my Lord the King, nosirree Bob."

"And those guys?"

Snurling, "Prophets. Don't worry about them. They dance. They sing. They say they speak for God. You ask me, good honest day's work's what they need. Pitchfork full of cow dung," said Mr. Smooth-Hands, "cure that bad case of glossolalia. Pick up the tips and tidbits still come Daddy's way, but fasting's still their shtick anyway. Loophole in the anti-fortunetelling laws: prophecy's allowed."

As Joel saw it, these ecstatics were interns, uttering their spiritual nonsense as a sort of audition should his father's position become vacant, achieving status within the racket before moving in and taking over. Should his father pass on, the son fully expected the prophets' ambition to bloom and flash into bloody flower. Only, the thing is, the old man's still-firm grip upon this last hill keeps these psalmsters innocent. Should temptation to power find outlet, their tumbles down the hill would break more necks; their flailings in the spirit would come to arms and hands that might have just, by chance, picked up a knife. One out of all these pure hearts, one who rapidly learns cunning, one with the most instrumental attitude toward his fellows: he will emerge into some corner of the great public space my father has hollowed out. Whatever authority he still holds, he holds by sheer force of character. Old guy hangs on by the fingertips, but fingertips more powerful than ten of these ascetic wraiths together. He could flick his pinkie, my daddy could, and skittle you all to far Naphthali. Take your seat upon his chair, and it crumbles to dust beneath you.

Poor soul. Neither Joel nor his brother Abbiah would ever know the elevation of spirit that daily breezed the garments of these prophets. While the soul-corrupted brothers walked through a world as trivially real as paperclips, these gamey fools sailed through worlds of purest spirit. God's will upholds all being, so divinity and revelation infuse all things: gnat, boulder, moon, hill, buttercup. All of them burn with His truth. Touch what seems mere matter while in the grip of such knowledge, and His warmth emerges from even the coolest marble.

Sharply pointed starlight can slice an eyeball, and in the proper mind, the taste of bread can unfold with complexity to rival $80-a-bottle wine. Bless all. Bless even hogs and clams as well, for they too, even the unclean, proclaim divinity; in squeal and squirt, they instantiate the profane, and so their oink and shell-click thereby eternally declare, "All else! All else is sacred!" All! Fart and falcon, toenail and Torah. (For what, indeed, is the world but penstroke upon penstroke of most Holy Writ?) Life's apex is to behold a brick and to know it as an expression of divine will: this particular roughness, this particular heft, this color, this misshapen edge, and this other particularly well-formed corner persist and endure, came into being and shall end someday by virtue of the Lord's own particular decision—a grain of divine will revealed now to me. To behold any single thing—I mean really behold it—is to behold Joy unending in all its depth. And to live in a world a-clutter with God's creation, the infinite detail of His will—well, it's more than a sensitive soul can stand. Even prophets' minds cannot encompass the ineffable, so the bodies those minds lived in shivered. Neither can language encompass the infinite, so it flames into poetry and burns away the mental walls. Verse into song and song into music that lends rhythm to the seizures, all shuffling them into a herky-jerky sublimity of dance. Bodies at one with the universe, they prophesied incoherently to all and sundry, offering promiscuously their infinite wisdom.

Who listened? No one.

Who would understand the jabber if they did? The same.

The breath of God, which fulfilled these very minor prophets utterly and smacked their lives into living glory, felt to Joel like a fly on his arm—a petty annoyance to brush off and forget. Not so for Soldiers I and II.

As the three approached: tabor and psaltery, harp and shepherd's pipe, bells and voices.

I: "This crazy music kids are into these days, I just don't get it. It's just noise. It's got to ruin their hearing, and it gets them hooked on incense. I see nothing wholesome about it." But his toe gets a-tappin'.

II: "The perennial alienation of youth seeks outlet in cultural expressions (e.g., clothing and music) designed to reject—either by inversion of some major element or exaggeration of some not-fully-incorporated element in the preceding generation's own initially rebellious cultural expressions—values which that same preceding generation has come to hold dear after their own period of youthful rebellion." And his fingers get a-snappin'.

I: "They say—like I can't see right through them—it's all innocent, doesn't mean anything, but I'll tell you what I've heard. I've heard it gets them into idol worship. If you write the words down, then read them backwards, skipping every other letter, they say one of these songs says, 'Bow to the Golden Calf.'" His legs start a-hoppin'.

II: "The reaction of the older generation, likewise, is predicated upon a denial of the rebellious elements in their own earlier cultural commitments. Having become historical, those elements of past rebellious youth culture are invested with the prestige of tradition and so can be associated with the whole archive of the established culture in contradistinction to the novelty of current rebellious youth culture, which itself is now, therefore, perceived as a threat to the entire edifice of tradition." And his head keeps a-boppin'.

I: "Here, try it yourself. Every other letter and backwards, from that one song, it goes, if you work it out, 'Full as cancer, dull orange hit out own orb.' No, that doesn't work. 'Full as....' That's not right. 'Full as a canker, dull as—' no, 'dull or agree'? 'Full as....' I'm getting this wrong. It goes....How does it go? I'm getting confused." Well, his tail starts a-waggin'.

II: "The nature of the threat lies not in the shifting modes of taste nor even precisely in the rejection of values, but in the perceived danger that culture, as a body of survival strategies in a communicable package will proleptically problematize into a....Wait. Communicable survival strategies. They will....There is a perceived danger that, uh,...shifting modes of taste...threat lies not in the nature of....I'm losing the thread." And his hips are like to shaggin'.

He's laggin'.

He's baggin'.

His throat starts gaggin'.

And his chest starts saggin'.

But then he catches the beat.

And he's shufflin' his feet—

Gloria in excelsis deo! The light broke upon their hearts, and worldly concerns evaporated into feeblest mist. They joined the dance of the prophets on the hillside. They sang with new voices and spoke with new tongues. They saw straight through the solid earth. And they were torn and whirled by a delight that would hurricane their lives away.

Until that moment when it suddenly departed. And then they found themselves abandoned into the quotidian, the ecstasy having lasted long enough to break them away from their earlier lives, but itself departing, leaving no instructions but the prophecies that evanesced like dreams.

Joel was impressed—amused, but still impressed. He got paid, after all, in advance.

Abbiah heard of the money to be made in being a plot device, and Joel, flush with delight at the windfall, didn't mind sharing the profits when the second pair of assassins needed a guide. And he specifically routed them past the prophets' hillside.

It turned out to be not a one-time fluke, but a sure deal. Any minimally susceptible mind picked up the contagion. You could watch them approach the Hill of the Prophets and lose their mission-directed focus. They'd slow down, they'd blink, they'd shake their heads, and they'd stop a moment to orient themselves before walking on again less steadily. Then eyes would lift, and their mouths would open singing. They would trip across some spiritual threshold, and a stumble became the first step of a dance. Samuel's boys watched the warriors lose their composure as the prophets descended the hillside—watched battle-hardened soldiers shudder, moan lowly, then raise a howl before they caught the prophets' melody and sang their minds away.

And a third pair! Off they go! Like clockwork. And the King's money just kept rolling in. How long could Joel and Abbiah keep it up?

"… any damn thing, you got to do it yourself," and other mutters less coherent still as the King himself rose to carry out his own orders.

The spy, having regretfully inured himself to the corruption around him, had by this time agreed to a kickback scheme whereby, for a consideration, he was to guarantee J & A Assassination Tours a continuing clientele of spiritually challenged killers. With the King now taking up the mission, the spy now steered in their direction the most spiritually challenged of them all.

Saul wondered could he do it. He wondered, had the others simply copped out on some phony religious exemption (or maybe they persuaded themselves they had a calling; it came to the same thing) so that they would not have to sneak up on the famous guerilla commander? They'd been trained on what to do when they got to Samuel's villa. Saul had now undergone the training himself:

Camouflaged, silent, knife at ready, through the window after midnight, identifying by feel the pallet described in the intelligence reports. Hand upon the window frame, the knotted wall hanging, bare foot upon someone's sandal, toe against a basket, then four steps to the right. Silent, silent, silent, silent. Bed linen. Leather pad in the hand ready to stifle his mouth. Blade low. Must be quick. Rehearse the act once more before committing to it. Still time to pad back out the window. Commit.

But Saul's mind wandered beyond the protocol. He would feel right at the moment of commitment a hand upon one's own wrist—feel it tighten, twist. Cold Philistine iron against my own throat. Pause. And then, he thought, my own blade in me, my own voice silenced by someone else's hand.—Can't blame them, the ones who balked. Reputation already gave David the muscles, stature, and intelligence of the Michelangelo. A giant among men. As in the valley of Elah, a kingdom balanced upon the willingness of a single warrior to face a mighty foe. But in this petty generation, where can we find Goliaths to fight our David? Who would feel he had a chance? Better to blow your mind on prophecy. Who can blame them?

Any case, what kind of leader sends boys to do a job he wouldn't undertake himself? My kingship ends today.

Part of the death wish: against Abner's advice, Saul had set off without a retinue. To his first meeting with Samuel, long ago, he had traveled with just one servant. Expecting this to be his last meeting with Samuel, he repeated the pattern. The same (now middle aged) man accompanied him. Abner quietly ordered a guard detail to shadow discretely.

Approaching Ramah, they came to the great well that is in Sechu, and Saul asked two gentlemen there, "Where are Samuel and David?"

Joel glanced toward the retainer with the moneybag, who nodded. "Naioth."

I know his place there. I know the guestroom my enemy would sleep in.

And as Saul walked, he began to contemplate his own heroism. No throne-bound delegator, here he was conducting the business of state himself. Samuel had said, long ago, "God will bring to your hand what you need to do, and you only need do it." My subordinates' inability has placed the task in my own hands. God blesses my whacking David. I don't know why He would so bless me, but I only need do it. Somehow, I am chosen, and it is something only I can do. No longer on a suicide mission, he stepped more lightly. David is simply a ram given me to sacrifice. I love that boy. He is my Isaac upon the mountain. What great love the Lord felt for Abraham to entrust him with that mission, he feels now for me. God saves the King after all. This vale of depression and unpopularity has been a trial I must pass through to demonstrate my worthiness. I walk through the Valley of the Shadow fearing evil in the guise of a shepherd boy. Only by the sacrifice of this son of Jesse, this new Isaac, shall a new era dawn. And I and my line shall be the uncontested rulers of a great dynasty. Samuel, in his mad jealousy, was wrong. I have in my sheath the sharp edge of the Lord's directly offered blessing. And today my kingdom shall have its true beginning.

Head full of this stuff, he felt an exultation such as he had not felt in years, ever since, why yes, this hill right here, where the prophets…and by George, here they…yes, this is exactly how it…oh praise the Name of the Lord! Yes, this is it! Look what he's done for me! Why I, I feel like dancing!

And so he did. Then he felt like singing, so he did that, too. And he felt like shouting, so he shouted. [A sound I won't produce phonetically. You'll have to buy the CD with my vocal performance of that shout and of other vocal music both integral and incidental to the story. $18.99 plus shipping, available separately since my negotiations to have the publisher bundle together the book and the CD seem to have bogged down. The publisher thinks people will love the book so much they'll want to buy the record separately. Me, I'm not so sure. I keep telling them, with the bundle, you make two sales each purchase; even with the discount, they're buying a CD most of them wouldn't otherwise buy along with it. And call this false modesty if you will, but I really don't think there's that much of a market out there for a recording of me singing the Davidic psalms, replicating Saul's ecstatic warble, and providing other vocal sound effects cued to specific passages in the text. This is the only way I will ever have anything close to that hit record I've always dreamed of. This writing gig is fine. Really, it is. But music is my destiny, and my spirit seeks room to spread my arms and spread my soul and sing!

Son, you've drawn too near that sacred hill. Come down.

Hm? I have. You're right. Where am I? Back to Saul.]

He had, all this while, been blowing his spiritual energy out a ramshorn that had somehow come to his hand. It echoed hosannas through the valleys. It bugled blessings unto all of Israel. Spontaneous melodies, inspired improvisations, whirling arpeggios! Such thrilling joy as he'd never known at being the Lord's own chosen. He wished to explain it, preach it, spread it to the sober-faced people now gathered around the hill, and a hymn of pure prophecy streamed from his mouth to wash blessings upon them all. Such a fire burns within me, the merest touch would crisp you all to holy cinders. Here, let me show you. [The King placed a hand upon a shoulder, and in return, the man he touched smiled.] Me, it consumes, and I flare the more, the fire its own ever-renewing fuel. Hosanna! Oh, this is what it is to be Chosen! Thus to be the Lord's own favorite! Thus to be a tool in His hand, the tool by which He carves the world unto His will! That His will should coincide with the fortunes of my house—such blessings He bestows upon my family! And he twirled and sang, dispensing the royal garments unto come-who-may, and he felt the wind upon his whole body as the divine breath, a bellows upon the blaze of his soul.

Joel, the cynic: "So since when is Saul one of the prophets?"

What? Who said that?

Someone: "Ha! You hear what he said? 'Is Saul, too, among the prophets?' What a gas!"

Who said that?

Everyone was saying it now.

It broke the spell. They were all laughing at him. He saw that he was naked, and he was ashamed. He wished to cover himself. The servant who had accompanied him saw to it. The shadow-guards just over the hillside cracked up laughing at it. And now all Saul could do was slink back home, humiliated in front of his former subjects. David was safe in Samuel's home.

Joel: "Not so bad for a lousy plot device, eh? Brought the episode to a nice round conclusion, didn't I?"

Thanks. You did a great job.

"'S been a pleasure doin' business with you."

Abbiah: "Wait. You had it all…?"

"Tell you 'bout it later. Be seein' you."

Bye.

17.

One day, Jonathan was walking along, minding his own business when—

"The f— Hey!"

Pinned on the dirt road, heard, "What have I done? Eh?"

Mouth full of dust, getting rolled and smacked into a wall, heard, "What's my crime?" Slapped across the face, he felt then tasted blood and heard, "What have I done? I'm asking you. What have I done?"

Said, "What have I done?" Spat.

"What have *you* done? What have I done? Why's he—"

"He?"

Throwing Jonathan back on the dirt like he's not worth the effort of beating up any further: "Dumb ass. Your father."

Picking himself up and, as a gesture of mourning and humility—also like he's never heard this before, "My father? God forbid that he should, you know, I mean…."

OK. All right. We'll deal with this now.

"He's grooming me, OK? Tells me everything. Doesn't always clear it with Abner even, but he tells me. Got to learn the ropes or something. And if what you're saying is true…" Fucker's gonna kill me: they both knew it. "This is big. This, he'd tell me."

David, pokerface, not buying it. Obviously not true. Jonathan is either lying or deluding himself. Poor guy. He's in love.

Which makes him useful.

"Jonathan," arm around his neck, kiss upon his cheek, "your father knows about us." And Jonathan jerked back, swinging his head left and right like he expected the old man to emerge from behind the bushes. "No, really, it's all right. He knows. So he wouldn't tell you. Maybe he just doesn't want to hurt you. Really. He loves you and wants you to be happy, so he's not going to tell you. This close, man, this close." Pinchy fingers.

Jonathan sidled up insinuatingly, "This close?" And said Jonathan unto David, "Whatsoever thy soul desireth, I will even do it for thee." A soulful look in his eyes. Really, Jonathan would do anything at all for David. Play out any fantasy, wrap his body, his tongue around any desire this beautiful boy might have. He burned to fulfill his loved one's needs.

"That's not it. Not now."

Here's the situation. Loopy as it may sound, even after that series of assassination attempts, Saul might consider the whole affair from spear toss to hillside prophecy water under the bridge. The man is not, after all, known for his emotional consistency. Saul might think David will recognize that his fit is past and be willing to return to an honored place at court. Might actually even expect his presence at the upcoming observance of the New Moon. (Jonathan nodded: yeah, that'd be like him.) Or—guy didn't get where he is today by being a total moron—he might act as though he fully expects and welcomes David's return, letting David assume the attempted murder was an aberration, a passing mania like so many others that seize the troubled king in his depression. Pay it no mind. He just gets that way sometimes. Let it go and settle back down into the ordinary routine of life at court. And then.

So here's the plan. Next day at the observance of the New Moon, Saul would ordinarily expect David there at dinner, right? But instead, David would hide out in the field, that one over there amid the bushes, hollow trees, and piles of rocks. He would hide there till the day after tomorrow. If Saul should at all remark upon David's absence, however innocently, Jonathan would say, "Oh, I forgot: he asked me if he could run down to Bethlehem for a big family reunion thing, big annual sacrifice they do down there. Meant to tell you. Sorry." If Saul would be cool with that, then life would return to as near normal as it can be under a manic-depressive absolute monarch. But if Saul should become angry at the news, then Jonathan could be sure that his father meant evil.

Hand upon Jonathan's shoulder, sliding around toward his neck, stroked the nape. With exquisite irony, considering who was dominant in this relationship: "Deal kindly with your servant. This bond between us…." He stroked Jonathan's chest with his other hand. Still scared of David's words, Jonathan felt all giddy. David had never touched Jonathan this way before, only allowed himself to be touched. "It was all your idea, you know." Brushing lightly across his nipples, ever so lightly, the breath of a tease. "So you have a responsibility." Brush your hand lower down my body. Please. But I cannot speak. "You made me your servant." My wish to be your servant. "So kill me."

Hm?

David backing off: "If you see evil in me, kill me."

Longing and fear: "No!"

"Why should you go to all the trouble of bringing me to your father? He thinks I deserve it? You do it yourself. Otherwise, what kind of son?"

Tearing.

"What kind of loyal son?"

"I just don't want to be cut off from you forever. I'll die."

"You won't die."

"Just promise me."

"You swear first."

"I swear. You're the one I'm faithful to. Always. Now you."

"I promise."

"Promise what?"

"Tell me."

"Even when the Lord has cut all your enemies off the face of the Earth, my house, you will not cut off."

This is what David had come for. That is what he wanted to hear. My rival submits. "Yes."

And that seemed to satisfy Jonathan, though just to be sure, as the story says, Jonathan caused David to swear again because he loved him, for he loved him as he loved his own soul. They arranged a time, a place, and a signal.

And Jonathan watched his father. That evening, at the traditional New Moon dinner, Saul made no reference to David, did not at all note his absence. Hoping for his friend's return to grace, Jonathan interpreted this non-observation as precisely such a sign. My father perceives his harpist's absence, yet attributes it, no doubt, to some random ritual uncleanliness. Can happen to any of us. This was, of course, a stretch, for it assumed Saul had tacitly expected David's attendance. And why should he expect the man he'd tried to murder to show up as a dinner guest? Watch *The Godfather* again and see how comfortably the Mafiosi let bygones be bygones. Even without seeing the movie, Jonathan knew this. Jonathan assumed his father would be thinking of David mainly because Jonathan himself could think of nothing else. His food tasted particularly well salted when he noticed it at all. Whatever the real David's charisma and good looks, the version Michelangelo would one day carve for Florence began to form that day in Jonathan's mind, more charming and handsome each moment the prince came closer to losing him.

At dinner on the second day, Saul broke his son's fugue state. As he was eating his mutton and chickpeas, "So your friend, Jesse's kid, yesterday, today, he's not here. What's up?"

"Oh, yeah, right, big family thing down in Bethlehem, annual sacrifice or something. His brother—I forget which one—he insisted."

Wiping greasy fingers upon his sleeves, setting aside his dish, setting aside explanation. Gave the eye to nearby courtiers who knew to back off, the man wanted to speak unheard. Quietly—this was for Jonathan alone—"You know the saying, don't you? Keep your—"

"Yeah, '… and your enemies closer.' I know it, Pop."

"Either way, whichever one he is, you don't just let him wander off into Judea, you understand? If he's close enough here to tell you that, you can keep him here." So he came back.

"What, like you did in Ramah, just walking away like that?"

"Now, that was different."

Cocked ears ablaze with useful gossip, courtiers now left altogether.

"Son, I need to explain politics to you. You know why I want him here?"

"You want to kill him."

"It's not quite that simple."

"You're jealous. I can tell you are. You're just jealous. That's what it is."

Divided loyalty. "You know who my successor would be, don't you?" Gesture, palms up: I'm handing it to you. "A dynasty protects itself from rivals."

"Ha! What dynasty? I don't need your help."

"Begins somewhere. Second one," gesture again, "takes the throne, it's a dynasty. Got to think of your own career prospects." For what it's worth, Saul explained, his own historical place was already secure: first in the list of Israelite kings. But who should be next, and whose progeny would succeed in glorious reverence through the ages? Jonathan's actions could determine whether Saul stood at the head of a great line, Jonathan a second who was to charge the tale with ever greater glory, or whether, as might happen, Saul would come to be perceived as a historical false start, a stuttering opening to someone else's epic. "History, m'boy, glory everlasting throughout the ages—not to be traded for a pretty set of buns."

Jonathan reddened something fierce. They are pretty!

"Look, son, you're married, and—"

"So what's your point?"

"I'm just saying—"

"So what's your point?"

"You have a, a posterity to worry about."

"Posterior? Cover my ass? Is that what you're saying? Somebody's pretty backside?"

"No," heating up, "you're twisting my words. You're evading your responsibility to the family."

Getting up, "'Is Saul among the prophets?' Ha ha! 'Saul has killed his thousands.' Ha ha ha! This is hilarious. 'Responsibility to the family.'" From the doorway, "Don't make me laugh."

Grabbing toward Jonathan and missing, "Little shit. What do you think you're doing?" And he stumbled over a cushion as he lurched doorward. Jonathan escaped who knows where, and King Saul was left in an undignified muddle on the floor. My son is loyal to his generation, and David is its leader. Way we could do it, it just occurred to him, is to let David see himself as the power behind the throne. Just like Samuel, and he fades off into irrelevance in the face of institutionalized office. Or even if he keeps Jonathan's dick in his pocket (and right away, he regretted the metaphor), King's Best Friend is not a hereditary office, and my dynasty persists beyond that one weak generation. So, thinking it through, Saul made himself feel a lot better. He wasn't even angry any more. All he needed was to get Jonathan to settle down, then explain to him and make sure he understood how David could be useful to them. Saul felt clear-minded and optimistic.

Jonathan stayed awake all night, and as soon as it was light enough, called a servant to accompany him on archery practice in the agreed-upon field. On a bowstring as tightly stretched as his heart, he pulled, aimed skyward, and felt the twang of exaltation as the shaft leaped high and far. Crying felt good, and he loosed another higher and farther. He was aiming at clouds. Tighter now, like his clenched teeth, and, "AAAH!"—shout it off on its trajectory.

Two deep breaths. The time had come to lose him.

"Fetch those arrows," he said more loudly and clearly than he needed to. "They landed off beyond that big rock." That was the signal.

And then the long wait while the lad trotted out into the field, found one arrow right away, then looked around, wandered among the higher weeds, peered about to distinguish arrowshafts from reeds and straight sticks, got fooled by shadows. Ah, there's one. Glanced here and there, came perilously close to the Hiding Rock, began a systematic scan of the ground, walking the field as the ox plows. Why did he pick such uneven ground? Nice even pastures just the other side of the—Ah! There it is. Then the leisurely trot back and the servantly proffer of the arrows.

Bobbing on the surface of his panic, calling up nonchalantly from within a widening pit of emptiness, "Oh, that's enough for today. Just head back without me."

All this way for three lousy shots? Spoiled aristocrat. And away he sauntered. Slowly.

Is he? Gone.

David stepped out, his face all wet, his cool gone in the two days of hiding—for even heroes fear death, and he really did love Jonathan. Now he bowed down before Jonathan as before an idol. "Thy servant I am! Oh godly generosity! In thy debt unto my farthest generation!"

"You were right!" Arms and hands all over David. "He went nuts. All I did was mention your name, and he went ballistic, totally blammo! He is going to kill you. Oh, David, he's going to kill you." Whimpering now, holding and caressing the one he loved. "Please, just this once. It would be the last...."

No.

But then one broke down in tears, and then the other one did, and they kissed and hugged and wept. Yes, they fondled one another's members, but this was not a sexy moment, so they stopped and just abandoned themselves to fear and mourning. David, ever cool under pressure, trusted that Jonathan had come alone, and so he felt free to loose his tears and feel all he was about to lose: status, influence, esteem, and, yes, his best friend. For all his calculation and manipulativeness—deep within his politician's soul—David felt in his heart a love for Jonathan. In years to come, he would be admired and adored; infatuated women would leap into his bed; historically unprecedented charisma would charm his people by the thousands; and each of his many wives and children, even his son Absalom the traitor, would show, at some point, though it would not last, a genuine affection for him: still, no such love—unqualified commitment from one who knows him to the depth and breadth and height his soul could reach—would he ever know again. Today, he was leaving the love of his life, who had saved his life in order to send him away.

18.

At this point, the danger is that David takes over the story and that Saul just fades, becoming the background for the younger leader's charismatic rise. Saul, in the usual version of the story, lays the necessary groundwork, clears out the old tribal order so that the new royal nationalist order might emerge. The triumphant story then depicts David's heroic rise in contrast to the hapless Saul's decline. That he has already begun to decline, that Saul's blessing has already flown, means that David's time is ripe. He can justifiably seize the power Saul has shown himself increasingly incompetent to wield. David will win the political struggle. A kingdom will point to *him* as its founder and tell story after story about his humanity and his greatness.

Posterity loves power so much that they recount even his crimes with affection. Who doesn't love the story about Bathsheba? It shows that the great man is only human; he had his faults, just like you and me.

But let's look at that story for a moment. Why has it been so popular?

Right alongside the King, we get to peep at the pretty neighbor in her bath. The first thought is not, What a creep. Here's a sin we smaller men can identify with. While his subjects, exposed to such a lovely sight, might then generally just jerk off in solitude, a king is not subject to the same restraints. According to Freud, you will recall, civilization depends on men's willingness to suppress the urge to grab every woman who arouses them. Society functions smoothly only because we all repress so much. Such rules, of course, do not apply to barbarian kings. Wouldn't we all love the power to just send for her? The story thus offers the vicarious satisfaction of sexual power. And what does Bathsheba herself feel? Who cares! She's the desirable object our hero gets to possess, and through him, we get her, too. Want him or not, she can't say no to the King, and better not reveal to her husband Uriah the source of that bulge in her belly. (Much, much later in David's story, she'll finally open her mouth. She'll push for the priority of her boy Solomon over the sons of David's other wives. Is this the expression of self-interested calculation that's been there all along since she soaped her chest out on a roof where she knew the King could see her, or on the other hand, has she, all these years, nourishing resentment, figured he owed her?) And that other thing Freud said we learn to do so that society might function smoothly: repress the desire to kill men who obstruct our desires—neither does that apply to ancient kings. We get to see David arrange for Uriah's demise, inconvenient husband of the woman he wants. David's hands are deniably clean: one wants the finest warriors at the front of the line, no? Here's the genius element in the story: make him a foreigner, a Hittite, not one of "us" anyway. Vicariously, we get to kill this alien in our midst. Sex, power, extirpation of the feared Other: this story has so many satisfying elements. And best of all, David, our hero, feels so guilty in the end. So we in the audience get to join the prophet Nathan, voice of the superego, in accusing him: little man, with the power of righteousness behind him, standing up to the great and prevailing. A kind of David and Goliath story, if you will. We get to indulge the id-ly satisfactions of an absolute monarch, yet still appease the superego by endorsing the curse upon the sinner. David is the name for the stories that satisfy us.

David's story has been taken up and magnified by religions of world historical importance. Saul's, one might argue, has been, too, since it precedes and interweaves with David's. He is known, sure, but not honored. He is the background against which David's honor shines. Donatello, Caravaggio, Michelangelo—great artists have loved the heroic young David. Saul? His greatest artistic embodiment is an oratorio by Handel (not too shabby, I know) in which, like some Old Testament Othello, his is driven mad by jealousy ("Saul has slain his thousands/And David his tens of thousands"). I see the root of the tragedy, however, not in jealousy, but in self-doubt. David's charisma and self-assurance are the bright background for the stark silhouette of Saul's insecurity.

If I identify with David, I fantasize about might and power, the social summit. Senators who absorb their economic notions via chats with CEO acquaintances come to base their thinking on the interests of the powerful. And if I gain too much satisfaction from David's story, then I risk seduction to a worldview that values conquest and authority. David is a dream of power beloved by its subjects: righteous, justified, divinely ordained. Power that understands itself that way is dangerous. It loves only the god that has blessed it with authority, not the weak whom it crushes on the road toward its godly aims.

Take, for example, David's appropriation of the threshing floor of Araunah the Jebusite on Zion Hill. The King himself approached the farmer. Talk about intimidation. One is sent for—not visited—by royalty. There was no protocol for Araunah to inhabit. Naked of protective ceremony, vulnerable, a conquered Gentile in an increasingly expansionist and nationalistic Jewish kingdom, he couldn't breathe. David wanted his barn (as if there were no others in the kingdom) for a holy sacrifice unto the Lord. And on this site, his offspring Solomon would build the Temple. In all pious intent, he stripped Araunah of his livelihood and of his patrimony. To secure at least his life, Araunah, breathing shallowly by now, offered the barn, the threshing floor, the oxen for the sacrifice, wood, flint, kindling, anything His Majesty might need or wish, anything. And the gift was refused. "I'll pay you for it." *I shall owe you nothing. You shall have no debt you can call in, no moral standing, no rights of victimhood. You shall have no recourse to another man's pity, no right to call upon your god or mine for vengeance, for you have been compensated. And you have alienated the land of your fathers now and passed it on to me and my posterity. Contemptible son who sells away your father's house for a jingle of shiny metal. Be shunned by your neighbors as a traitor to your conquered people.* So Araunah heard and, as though he had a choice, accepted.

If I identify with Saul, I avoid the seduction of power. As he lacked the preparation and aptitude for his authority, I must admit my own lack on my much smaller scale. With Saul, I lack the incentive to forget myself and to identify instead with the hero. He offers little in the way of vicarious satisfaction. With Saul, I stand not in the company of serene dominion, but with an ordinary man thrust forward beyond his realm of competence. If I identify with Saul, the lowly who are harmed by careening power do not fade from view as the chariot speeds onward toward Destiny. I stand with Saul and the other pedestrians. And while Saul himself may stand uselessly and enviously staring after those swift horses of secure monarchy, I might—because I stand in the road and not mentally inside the chariot—I might see and record in my book the broken and the dead.

And sure, he committed enormous crimes such as the Amalekite genocide, but—

There is no but. The ethic of the time is no excuse. He deserves no honor.

On with his story.

19

All right. One David story, just one, and then I get right back to Saul. OK? This is one of my favorites, from his days as an outlaw.

Once upon a time, there was a particularly wealthy man in Maon known by the name of Nabal. (Handel wrote an oratorio about him, too. What does this pattern tell us about Handel, that he wrote about the morally compromised losers to David?) And one day, he was visited by a contingent of ten young men in fedoras and in dark suits with wide lapels and broad shoulders. "Nice place you got here," observed one of these gentlemen, without performing the courtesy of removing his dark glasses. "Seem to be doing just fine for yourself here, just fine. And hey, you know?" he added, picking up and admiring, without invitation, a particularly expensive looking vase. "I very much hope you should always keep on doing just fine. Know what I mean?" Meaningful glance over the top of his shades. "My employer has requested that I inform you, since you seem to have been unaware of it," setting the vase down with exaggerated care, "that we have never roughed up or in any way even seen cause to maltreat any of the shepherds in your employ, not a digit upon a one of them. We have," absent-mindedly cracking his knuckles, "treated your entire livestock operation in the Carmel vicinity with the greatest of delicacy and respect. Your own inventory records should indicate to you zero loss in the Carmel area due to pilferage. You don't need to look it up. We make it our business to know. In fact, you might be interested in learning, if you were not till this point cognizant of it, that we have informed other interested parties in the area that, should any (and I sincerely hope not) of your people be harmed or should any of your property be so unfortunate as to turn up missing, we would hold them personally responsible, as though," gesture, tossing it off as a trivial point, "it was our very own."

Pause. Nabal, pudgy little bald guy, type-A personality, was fuming. Two beefy suits outside the door, one inside it, one at each window, one by the door to the back room, two more in the back room just to look around. So far now, he just fumed.

"And our employer, David—perhaps you've heard of him?—he thinks you have perchance been awaiting an opportunity for a display of gratitude. He has instructed me that I should accept," leaning forward, unseen eyes drilling through the dark lenses, "whatever tokens you should care to offer. With gratitude, I mean, unto thy servants and to thy son David."

Nabal had now had more than he could stand. "David? Who is this guy? Who the fuck is the son of Jesse, and where does he get off demanding anything of *me*? I've sweated blood to build up what I have here today, and you punks demand a piece of it," slamming his soft fist into his chubby palm. "So you didn't steal, you didn't hurt anybody. Good, good. You know what? YOU'RE

NOT SUPPOSED TO!" Pleased with himself for clinching the argument with that one. "You want some reward for that? Huh? I don't get it." Muttering, not entirely to himself, meaning to insult, "Runaway slaves behind every hill these days. Whatever happened to respect for authority, commitment to your station in life? Never know who you're dealing with." No rise from them. "So let me get this straight: I should take *my* bread and *my* water and *my* meat, my own lovingly raised livestock I've tearfully slaughtered only for the sake of *my* shearers so they'd have something good to eat to keep their strength up while *they* are doing *work* for *me*—compensation for work, you know what that is?—and instead I should give it unto men whom I know not whence they be?" Staring them down: you couldn't intimidate Nabal.

With cool relish, "Very well. I shall relay this information to my employer."

Meanwhile, one of Nabal's own servant boys in that back room, who had seen the intruders and heard the conversation, ran to tell the gnomish rancher's strikingly beautiful wife. He felt ashamed to approach her: she was so gorgeous, and he so shamefully smitten with a married woman above his station. But he had to save her. She needed a hero. And I shall be the one.

Right away, she got it.

(And it would not have occurred to her to reward her little savior with a kiss.)

And David, too, got Nabal's reply. "Gird ye on every man his sword." And they decamped toward Nabal's homestead.

Right away, she got it. She got bread and wine. She got mutton, grain, and fruit cakes, dried fruit, fresh fruit. She got anything, anything in the larder. She got the servants to move with unprecedented celerity and silence. She got scary and commanding. She got to use her organizational intelligence as never before. She got razor eyes. She got logistical brilliance. She got warrior goddess demeanor. She got fear of death electrifying her spine. She got devastating beauty and a tragic mind.

She got it all loaded on donkeys behind her husband's back, over the ridge and out of his sight, on the road to meet the others who would kill them all. For David, everyone knew, led an army of the dispossessed, the poor and resentful, who, at the home of a wealthy man, would, given the order, gladly kill the owner and then pillage all he had owned, then rape the dead man's women—herself, she knew, the greatest prize.

David, on the path around the mountain, saw them coming, saw the donkeys. He was pleased. He wouldn't show it, of course, but he was very pleased. From behind his Angry Barbarian mask ("For this? For this, I guarded his property in the wilderness? Huh? From the wolves? I'll show you a wolf."), he appraised this woman. Comely indeed. (Coming in close, quietly threatening her face: "All his stuff out there: is anything missing? I'll tell you what's missing.") Not your slender girl, but a fully-formed woman (Snarling the sword tip close to the ear he spoke to: "Gratitude. He trades me evil for my good."), eloquently curved. He could tell by the fall of the robes over her prostrate form. And walk into those eyes, raised toward him for just a moment, wet with terror. A wide-souled, mature human being lives in there. (Heavy-footed circling with his drawn sword, as though calculating where to stab her first: "May God—I swear—may God be as good to my enemies,") Tall. ("if I get to this guy's house") I want to see her naked. ("and I leave, of all that pertain unto him") I want to see her hair. I can only guess from those eyebrows: a dark, dark brown. ("in the golden glow of tomorrow morning's dawn") Yes, here is a woman to wake with in the morning and to live with. ("a single one left to piss against a wall.")

Abigail, too, wore a mask, yet the one she selected fit her like skin: fear of violent death expressed via groveling abasement. Face in the dirt, shallowly breathing, tasting dust, hugging the ground, dear mother, to protect her, arms ahead toward the outlaw chief, empty: I am at your mercy, protect me, you have all the power. "My fault. Entirely my fault. Let all the punishment fall on me. Just listen to me. Please. Forget Nabal. He's a fool. It's all my fault. Your servants, I didn't see. I should have seen the men you sent. Seeing as how the Lord—you haven't killed anybody yet. He's stopped you, kept you out of guilt. I mean," back pedaling, "not that you'd be at all in the wrong. I mean, perfectly rightful vengeance. May it be to all your enemies as to Nabal." (Ah, he thought, so she means....) "And look, I've brought you an offering, for you and your men. I've brought it, your handmaid." (So does she also mean...?) "Forgive me my trespasses. God will make your house strong because you fight his own battles, and evil hath not been found in thee all thy days." (Yeah....) "We know who is after you. We know it is not me." (We know it isn't Nabal either, but that doesn't matter. Right now, this is not about my father-in-law.) She remained prostrate, but finding herself not yet dead, she spoke more deliberately now into the soil. "Your soul, the Lord holds warm, a shiny nugget in his pocket; the pebbly souls of your enemies, he'll nestle in his sling and fling them out." She looked up now. "You're going to be King. I know it. I want to be on your side. When this is all over, remember me." (Oh, I will.)

"OK, you've convinced me. They can piss against walls all they want. You did the right thing, kid. Thanks for the food." And he gave her his cute little smile, and she gave him hers. No, they did not wink.

What a woman.

When she got home, she found her husband feasting it up: rack of lamb, barley risotto, lightly wilted greens salad with a fruity vinaigrette, and wine, lots of wine. "You believe this guy?" he was saying to her as soon as she came in. "'I've never stolen from you, so I deserve some reward.' You believe that? I should give everybody who's never thieved from me some kind of payment. Can you see me going door to door, every farmer from here to Tyre, handing him a copper because he's done me the service of never robbing me? Flag down Bedouin caravans, make sure they all get their reward for ignoring me. Special messenger to Babylon, bag o' gold to divide among everybody who can prove he's never kidnapped any of you guys." Wine cup gesture toward the servants, who stood in stone-faced agony. "'Where were you on the night of August 5?' 'Didn't hurt nobody.' 'Good lad, here's a chit. Turn it in at the tavern for a drink on me. Doin' good work.'" Man, he thought he was funny. "Abbie, my little cuddle bun, c'mere."

One last undignified squeeze of her bottom to tolerate.

"Dear, your cup is empty. Have some more." Sit through minutes of the old man's cleverness, and repeat.

"Oh," as he greened, "I need to lie down."

She knew about his heart, so she waited till morning. At his bed, "Nabal, we need to talk." Ominous words always, they sprung him up. A heart, beating way too fast pounded pain into his wine-soaked head. He stomach squeezed to life and (he twisted and bent—amazing exertion) emptied into a bowl beside his bed. Ah, as he spat, that's better. And he heard his wife say, "Four hundred men descending upon the ranch to burn and kill." He felt that left-arm pain he'd felt before (she knew this), and then his chest seized up as it never had before, a muscle tearing deep inside. Each heartbeat hurt so much he dreaded the next.

"Rest, dear. Lie down. You need to rest." The Lord Himself hath turned my husband's heart to stone. Oh, blessed be His name.

And, good wife, she nursed him for a week and a half before he died.

And when David heard the news, he thanked the Lord for killing his enemy so that David himself would not have to commit that sin. The Lord is my hit man.

And Abigail, he did remember, and she, with her ruthless intelligence, became, ahead of his other wives Michal and Ahinoam, his favorite—until she was older (though he was, too) and he watched Bathsheba bathing naked on a rooftop.

20.

Enough of David. As I said, this is not his story. Back to Saul now.

He sat under a tree in Gibeah, spear in his hand. He'd taken to holding this spear, the one he'd thrown at his young rival. Heavy, well-balanced: power abided in this iron-tipped stick. I lift this deadly shaft, and I hold power.

"So why wasn't I told? He deals with the Philistines, he raises an army of malcontents, he hides out in the wilderness of Judeah. Evacuates his family. A man is loyal to his family, his tribe. Look," gestures. Quietly to the inner circle, drawn near, "You think he's going to reward you guys from Benjamin? I tell you, a guy like this, so much for rewarding you—he's going to take your seed, your vineyards, and your sheep, and he'll give them to his own officers and servants. He'll take your servants, your finest young men, and your donkeys, and he'll set them to do his own work. Conservative estimate, I'm saying he'll take a tenth of everything you own; realistically, this is a winner-take-all struggle, and we need to keep him isolated."

Then, they saw the dark spirit that he'd held off with that spear settle back upon him and recast his face. His brain chemistry, swiftly as cloud shadow, dimmed by one shade, and (to mix a metaphor here—synesthesia a symptom of some forms of depression) it savored now suddenly of a more bitter flavor. "Nobody's on my side. Who feels sorry for me in all of this? None of you even told me he'd turned my own son's head." Another shift, colors a shade darker still, but more sharply outlined, flavor more bitter yet. "My son turned my servant against me, didn't he? He's the one. And some of you knew about it." He eyed their poker faces.

Doeg, one among the more blighted of souls at the court, had bided his time these many years. Saul, afraid of him, had made the man his chief herdsman, a job that took him away from the court and off into the hills for much of the year. Doeg, a foreigner from Edom, followed power, service to power ever the approved outlet for the violent. He saw now his chance.

"I've seen him."

His Majesty's eyebrows rose with a positive life. The chemicals shifted again, but now toward a brighter taste.

"I saw him come to Nob, to Ahimelech the Priest, the son of Ahitub."

"Yeah?"

"Dig. Ahimelech inquires of the oracle for him, just for David. And dig this: gives him Goliath's sword. And dig still further and deeper, man: he feeds him with the show bread, bread of the sacrifice, bread of offering to you dudes' god that only the priests eat and only when it's stale. Only your sky god gets the freshness of it, I am led to understand, yet ben Ahitub takes it upon himself to sustain some outlaw with its nutriment. Crazy."

Bring him here.

Joy.

Ahimelech and all his family were brought to Gibeah.

"So, thou son of Ahitub."

"Here I am, Lord!"

"You've conspired against me with the son of Jesse. Bread, a sword, oracles. You've joined the insurrection. What do you have to say for yourself?"

Now, Ahimelech was a company man, one who had risen high, but still basically an attendant lord, one that will do to swell a progress, start a scene or two, advise the prince; deferential, glad to be of use, politic, cautious, and meticulous; full of high sentence, but a bit obtuse. Imagine Prufrock, Oriental priestly regalia not quite covering his high collar, flannel trousers, and bald spot, standing before the King accused of treason.

"That is not it at all! That is not what I meant at all!"

"I'll be fair. You needn't fear. Tell me what you meant."

Do I dare, and…do I dare? Sincerity is no protection, truth no evidence. But I am compelled to speak.

"Majesty, this is what I know. Who is so faithful among your servants as David, the King's own son-in-law, who travels at your command and does your bidding, and finds honor in your house?"

Saul wondered, why did Ahimelech phrase this as a question? The priestly speaker was gropingly tentative, but the royal listener heard not an evasion, but a challenge: Is anyone, anyone at all, any more loyal to you than David is, David the traitor? Do you think you have a following? You walk a solid-looking bridge of rotten timbers. None will support you when you stumble. Look around you: all will poke and shove you toward the deep and stony ravine.

"Did I inquire of God for him?" Did I? Try to remember. What did I do when he came to me? "Far be it from me. That would be utterly inappropriate, a breach," swell of professional pride, "of protocol. Not him. Not one so low. Even him. I saw Your Majesty's servant come, and I did serve Your will in him."

So he admits it: feeding, arming, and advising my enemy on the run.

Doeg's evil grin, Saul's hardening scowl, guards inching closer to him. A bloom of sweat and shorter breaths. "I didn't do anything wrong, nor any of my family. I promise you. I knew nothing of this." His words bunched in the air before his mouth, and they smothered him.

How does he know what to deny? And the King said, "Ahimelech, thou shalt surely die, thou and all thy father's house."

Ahimelech: knots cut into my wrist, and I am helpless to snip them. They bind my chest. No one has touched me yet with anything but words.

To the guards: "Kill all the priests. They're all for David anyway. You." The guard: Me? Oh, my goodness! "Turn around. Start with him," with Ahimelech.

Shuffle. Oh, well wouldn't you just know? I've never been in such a, such a pickle! And the eyes darted to the next guy, his partner.

Classic dilemma for us, if you think of it, the partner reasoned. State oppression of recalcitrant religious authorities. And in a sense, I represent a populace forced to choose. My actions will stand to history as theirs. And if I stand still enough, I just might become invisible.

"Hey, Pops, you got the bread, I got the": Doeg.

Royal nod. Draw your knife. Turn around.

"Crazy." This commission pleased him.

And swift as a stab through an arras, Ahimelech was gone.

This was so easy. He just stood there. Sure, it takes one hard shove through the gut with these crumby Israelite knives, but it was like he popped and deflated. I could do this all day. It's like bubble wrap. Press it in, tense as the sinews resist, and then bang! he's gone.

And he did do it all day when Saul sent him to Nob, a levitical city, to kill all the priests.

I have observed the rituals. Their meaning lies not in any godly favor but in their performance, nor disfavor for the marred or neglected ceremony. Their meaning lies only in themselves.

David improvised. To grieving Abiathar, Ahimelech's son: "When I saw Doeg there, I knew he would tell Saul. That's right. I knew this was coming, and I, in cowardly fear for my own safety, took your father's assistance, and I did nothing to help him. It's all my fault. I owe you more than I…I ought to pay…just got to…really I've…. Oh, Abiathar! Oh, it's too much! Oh!" He wept, and he drew the young priest close to him in a great iron grip of a hug. It was the warm embrace of a bar securing a cell door. Soppy, "Stay with me. I owe you safety. The same enemy is after us both. I will protect you. I will guard you."

The ambiguity of this guardianship welled in Abiathar like acid reflux, and he sank. He would hold his breath until it staled. And then he would rise. He would, in time, say to himself, "If I do not learn to surf, I drown." And so, a priestly endorsement, as though by merit, would fall upon the rebel.

21.

(We shall here omit several repetitious incidents of Saul and David, with their respective armies, chasing one another around and around the kingdom.)

Abner: "New intelligence."

Saul: Mumble, roll over, squint into the open tent flap.

Abner: "David is—"

"Oi."

"We've learned the kid's gone into the mercenary business, made a deal with the Philistines."

Up now, legs over the side. This is important.

"He's not attacking us."

Course not.

"But they're using him against some of the smaller Canaanite settlements."

Sure, but that frees up—

"Which frees up Philistine regulars to use against us."

"They've got a big build-up at Shunem."

"Yeah."

"So."

"Yeah."

They both just stood there a while.

"If I could persuade Samuel to support me on this—"

"Died a couple years ago, boss."

"Yeah, I know, but—"

"You made that illegal. Remember that deal with the priests, back when we were dealing with the priests?"

"Yeah, but—"

"PR disaster, I'm telling you."

"Look, it's not like I'd have to visit the witches myself."

Abner: ironic eyebrow thing.

"You know, plausible deniability."

The eyebrow settled down, but Abner was still giving him the look.

"So I'd have to go myself, you think?"

"Pssshhh," flailing arms, what-can-I-do-with-this-moron gesture.

"What?"

"Where?"

"You got any leads? Maybe somebody knows somebody."

"I'll see what I can do," but still, the look.

Abner poked his head into the guardroom, looked around the squad, and then nodded. "You two." Same two guys as always. Abner's head jerked toward royal headquarters.

Walking along, "We've sent you two on classified missions before. What do you know about disguise?" He glanced at the first one, who glanced at the second one.

And then they were in the Royal Presence, who said, "So what do you suggest? I used to be a peasant, you know. I think I can remember how to do it. You're the experts. How do I start?"

And Guard Number One felt bloom in himself a possibility he could not name, but we call it drag, and it pleased him at a level he had never before felt.

A world opened up to him, its first manifestation peasant drag for royalty.

"Oh, Your Majesty, no, no, no. That goatskin satchel is a dead giveaway. His Majesty is just trying too hard. Really now, leather is what you need. Here, let me help. A little lower on the—. Yes, that's right. Ooh. Oh yes. Very nice." He admired and thought, who shall I be now?

"Authenticity": Soldier Number Two. "That's the key." An external shell of costume that bears little relation to the internal representation of "self" becomes an occasion for dissonant social interactions as others note the class-bound bearing of the body clash with class-indicative signs of the habiliment. Lacking straightforward cues as to social status, one's interlocutors become likely to mark the dissonant actor as outside the class-based codes of social behavior. "Don't want to draw attention."

But his friend had just awakened to the beauty of artifice. "Oh, but someone just coming in from the meadows might have wildflowers dangling from the buskins. And look, pull the tunic forward a smidge, a little bit more so it shows some collarbone…. Yes. Isn't that just the look?"

"It's a look, all right."

Saul took note. These guys were the experts. Don't draw attention, flowers in the boots, show collarbone. "OK, you guys come with me."

Now, it's not like the Israelite army had uniforms in those days, just armor for some of the leaders. But you could tell who was who in battle pretty easily because each little nation (each tribe, for that matter) had its own distinct style— dye patterns, cut of the tunic, thickness of belt, hat shape. A high degree of local conformity contrasted with equally high diversity of styles between cultural units. Saul had needed help because he had not for years dressed as an ordinary Benjamite. So the guards didn't change clothes, just brought along their swords. Saul, however, felt as self-conscious as he had when he first became king. I wear clothes not my own on a mission that ill becomes me.

So three guys—one of them, frankly, rather poofty looking with those flowers in his boots—approached the cave-home of a reputed witch at Endor.

They heard, as they trod carefully through the undergrowth, "Bubble, bubble, toil and—"

Twig crack.

More loudly now, "And a teaspoon of oregano."

Saul, overcome with uncertainty, "Lady!"

Out of the darkness, "Um, just a minute! I'm, uh, just getting out of the bath!" A rustling sound, bump and clatter of kitchen equipment, something pouring in thick glugs. With a high, singing, innocent, "Who is it?" the old woman emerged, towel wrapped around clearly dry hair.

"Lady, I seek your help."

"My help? Oh, pish! What can an ordinary old woman like me do for such a," weird clothes on this guy, "fine gentleman?"

Akh! Help! She can tell I'm not a peasant! And I followed instructions exactly! She must be a witch! Ah, wait, but that's what I wanted. So. Deep breath. "OK. Huh. This is really important to me. I'll pay you. I need you to, uh...."

Poker face. Could be a trap, could be just a really incompetent undercover man, these other two his trainers or something. Old for a trainee. Maybe this guy's for real. Still dangerous—get what they need, then kill me to cover their tracks. Careful.

"Hooh, boy. OK, here goes. I understand you have a familiar spirit you work with. I was wondering if your colleague would be willing to contact a dead one I will name."

"That would be illegal."

And the guards thought, Weird shit. Nobody told us about this.

"You know what Saul's done: put all the wizards and necromancers out of business. Are you trying to trap me, Mister? You want me dead and hanged for some reason? You know what they do to witches—not just witches, people accused, suspected of witchery? Eccentric old women people just wonder about? Now, you stop it. All it takes to burn me is you get some rumor started."

So it dawned on Saul: Not just my own life in danger. I am risking yours as well.

Kneeling, "Lady, I apologize. I was thinking only of my own skin and the advice that I need from, from—"

"From beyond."

"Yes. I am a man of some influence, and it's pathetic, but I fear the loss of all that has come to me. I enjoy the command of many men, and I fear losing them. I have a comfortable home, and I eat well, and I fear losing that good life. I have enemies, and now I learn that they have joined together against me. The Lord has blessed me, and I have learned that He has withdrawn His blessing and has abandoned me. I am increasingly alone, and I may tell you I have been chosen for a special curse. One I look to for advice despised me in his lifetime, but no one else can tell me what to do."

Poor man.

Getting up, turning to go, "I was wrong to come. No harm shall come to you. I'll tell no one." To the guards, "You'll tell no one." To her again, bowing, "I swear by the God who plans my ruin, yet whom I honor still, no punishment shall come to you."

Poor man. "Wait. I know what it's like to be an outcast. Poor man. I can't help everyone, but I can help some. Only the truly desperate come to me for refuge."

She returned to the fire by the cave's mouth. She scraped some ashes from the edge of the pit, then dusted them over the trampled dirt of her fore-cave living area. With a stick, she drew a circle in the ash, then plucked a leaf from the nearby herb bed. (It was dark; they couldn't see the plant.) Placing the leaf upon her tongue, she spoke: "My friend, I need your help again."

A hollow voice, starting faint, growing loud: "I cannot soothe my own pain; I can only ease the suffering of others."

Smiling toward her guests, "She always says that. Now," placing a leaf on Saul's tongue—a dark green, bitter flavor, "don't swallow it. Go to the circle, and whisper the name. I don't need to hear it."

One of the guards (doesn't matter which, they both were scared, one more simply and purely, but the other just as deeply): "Is that a devil?"

"Of course. You can't work with angels. I've tried. They're ruthless. All they know is what's right, and they've got no sympathy for us poor humans always making mistakes. Got no pity. You can't count on them. One little thing, and they cut you off. Now devils, they know suffering. They made their mistakes, and they've been paying for it. Devils—a lot of them, anyway—can empathize. They understand. They know abandonment. They understand how much you need to count on them."

Quietly, Saul said, below the threshold of anyone else's hearing, "Samuel."

And he appeared. The great man, lost, fear in his eyes. "Aa!" Turning around, seeing living people, "Iiiiih! Hhhah!" This was not the Samuel of old who could command kings and fell oxen. This was a frightened soul—just the bare soul, no body to empower it now.

The witch, flinching back, too, atremble at this ghost, one she had not expected. To Saul: "You lied to me. I know who you are. No one else would—"

Saul: "What do you see?" In the dark above the ashen circle, he saw nothing.

The witch saw more than only Samuel. "Oh Lord! The old gods! A spirit that great, he cracks the mantle open. There, look! You let them out. What will happen to me now? Oh, the poor earth, all the people!"

Samuel, mouth stretched wide, eyes slit closed, and neck ascending upward: "AAAAH!"

"What shape," Saul asked, "does he come in?"

"An old man comes up, and he is covered in a shroud."

And now, by the moonlight, Saul could see dimly, and he stooped his back in reverent submission, and then he bowed. Yes, it was Samuel, to whom he owed homage.

"Huhn. AAAAH! WHY?" Down then to a suffering whimper, "Why did you hurt me? Why did you bring me up?" The old man cried vaporous tears.

And Saul felt pity for the suffering ghost, as he had once before felt pity for the living man on the hill at Gilgal. *I cannot know what I've done to him, tearing his soul from its rest, ripping him from an earthly womb into bodiless rebirth. An infant howling out its earliest breath, you don't ask it for political advice. I'm sorry. But I owe him an explanation.* "I am sore distressed, for the Philistines make war against me, and God is departed from me and answereth me no more, neither by prophets nor by dreams; therefore, I have called thee, that thou mayest make known unto me what I shall do. No one will say, and I know of nowhere else that I might turn. I apologize. I did not know that it would make thee to suffer." Before the specter of greatness brought so low, of pain so great, even his own penchant for self-flagellatory suffering fled, his own shame beside the point.

Samuel looked around, confused, head and eyes jerking about, hands grasping at some fleeting lucidity. "God's your enemy? And you make me join you? Why would you do this to me?" He flinched as though a bat flew at his face, notional hand up to protect his lost eyes.

"Samuel—"

Hands down, whining shout right at Saul: "Why do you do this to me? David has your kingdom already. Why do you go on?" Collapsing on himself: he had no energy. The dead have no energy. "It was the Amalekites. You didn't. I didn't. You didn't." Samuel's face showed the full weight of an emotion he had never felt in his righteous life: guilt. *I should not have confirmed and reconfirmed this weak man as king. I should have remembered Abraham and stood up to a god who makes mistakes. This is not the right man, Lord. Pick another. I'll keep the oil in my pocket till you do. But I—I of all people—followed blindly.* To himself, faint as an echo: "You did not do as you should."

Tomorrow. "Tomorrow," Samuel then said, "the Philistines win. And you— Oh! I don't want to know this! You call me back and make me know! You will join me," as though the ashen circle were a hole, it sucked him down, "here."

Saul, who had neither eaten nor drunk the whole night, nor the day before, fell down and wept. The crying felt good. As a baby cries in distress and, in time, comes to associate the tears with the approach of the mother's comforting ministrations, so that crying of Saul's became a comfort in itself, so Saul, shedding adult masculine reserve that could no longer serve him, cried and cried.

Poor man. The witch's fear for the world at the hands of the earth gods let loose that night condensed into pity for this one poor man. *I cannot save the nations, but I can feed one hungry king.* "Your Majesty, behold your handmaid. I have put my life into your hand, and I have this night obeyed your word. So now, I pray you, hearken also unto me, and allow me the honor to set before you a morsel

Shibboleth

of my own bread, and may it please you to eat it so that you may have strength as you go upon your way."

And he shook his head, still bawling on the ground.

Guard: "Master, please eat. You'll need your strength for the march back to camp."

Guard: "Master, creature comfort in the moment of your need—don't turn it down. Whatever you are served, surely it shall prove more savory than any banquet."

The witch: "For your men's sake, lest they should have to carry you."

For them. I should not be a burden. "All right."

And while Saul waited, drained of all emotion, staring into the ashen circle of his fate, the woman kneaded and baked unleavened bread (the Bible says she killed a calf, but I don't believe it—there would not be time for the butchery and roasting) and brought them strips of dried meat.

They ate it, rose, and walked away while it was still night.

22.

The part about the calf is, of course, not the only part I don't believe. I don't believe in ghosts, in witches, in the old gods the legend says the witch says she saw, or in Samuel's god either.

The whole story of Saul is pretty dubious and full of contradictions. Historians and archeologists have found no independent corroboration that there was a Jewish king so early nor any by that name. There may have been some leader of more or less that name whose shabby chiefdom morphed through legend into a kingdom, and no independent record of him remains because, like most little tribes, his left no concrete trace upon the landscape. No palaces, outposts, fortresses, or regal insigniae survive from this supposed reign. Sure, the random mutability of history has destroyed evidence of many great patches of time, and the Saulide kingdom, whatever its extent, just may be one of them. It happens. But then, it makes the reliability of the legend something we just can't know.

He could be, on the other hand, a folkloric invention entirely, a foil for the more glorious legend of David, whose success is made to shine more vividly out of Saul's great failure. Saul performs the further narrative function of assembling a kingdom for David to take over.

Or his legend may be more like the English Arthur's: some seed, planted at one of history's recordless intervals, blossomed in the telling, my own version just the most recent flower. The oral tradition branched, swerved, and looped back on itself, the limbs unaware of one another as they grew. Thus, three stories of how Saul got to be king: 1.) the anointment at Ramah, 2.) the nationwide council of selection, and 3.) his initiative in grasping the reigns of leadership to save Jabesh, where the people rewarded him with permanent command. Or for another example of how the branches of the oral tradition lose track of one another, Saul wiped out the Amalekites—all of them, even the babies, even the animals (barbarism to be proud of in the Bronze Age; in the Silicon Age, we cannot forgive it)—but later, when David was working as a mercenary for the Philistines, he battled the Amalekites, who had raided the Philistine town of Ziklag. And before the story is over, we'll meet one more living Amalekite. When, for a further example, did Saul first meet David? Here again, three stories: 1.) when Saul needed a musician to help lift his spirits, 2.) when the smart-mouthed kid visited his soldier-brothers at the front, or 3.) after the victory over Goliath. In all these places, and a few others, to ask, Which is it? is to mistake the nimbus of oral tradition (shiny mist around a bright center) for history. Scribes heard this, they heard that, and then they heard another, and fearless of the philosophic bugaboo of contradiction, collaged them all upon the page. They're all good stories. Why force tellers to pick just one?

What, then, happened? I feel free to elaborate, to take liberties, tell it a new way, knit together or shuffle the irreconcilable versions that the Bible leaves separate, because I don't know. Nonetheless, I've tried to be faithful.

His name, *Sha'ul* seems related to the word for "ask," *sha'al*. (I do not know Hebrew. I get this from Robert Alter's *The David Story*.) What should I do? Or (Alter again) "lent." What is given me is not mine.

A passage that I used in writing my Chapter 6: "[36]And Saul said, Let us go down after the Philistines by night, and spoil them until the morning light, and let us not leave a man of them. And they said, Do whatsoever seemeth good unto thee. Then said the priest, Let us draw near hither unto God. [37]And Saul asked counsel of God, Shall I go down after the Philistines? wilt thou deliver them into the hand of Israel? But he answered him not that day. [38]And Saul said, Draw ye near hither, all the chief of the people: and know and see wherein this sin hath been this day."

Characteristic moment: Saul asks God what to do and gets no response. The Job story, if he'd known it, would have told him that sin had nothing to do with it. God does not turn his back only upon sinners. That does not mean, of course, that Saul, the barbarian chief, was no sinner, only that it doesn't matter. He got no sign and interpreted that silence as fault, guilt to be atoned.

What did he expect? A gentle butterfly's-wing puff of breeze whispering, "Yes," to him alone? Or maybe, "No"? An augurable flight of birds? A voice rumbling out of the sky, dripping red rain, "Kill for me! I, the Lord your God, thirst for human blood! Now kill for my thirst! Kill!" Or some still small voice within him directing him toward the right?

Why did he expect anything? I am awed by Saul's faith.

23.

The Philistines were routing the Israelites around Gilboa. The whole army was collapsing. Weapons and armor, loads lightened in panic, littered the grass. Scattered across the stones and corpses, Philistine arrows sprouted like tough weeds. Ari and Ben (now, as an epitaph, I will give my two soldiers names) lay in one another's arms. An arrow had shot through the side of Ari's throat, and Ben, while the friend he loved choked on blood in his shattered windpipe, held him, stayed with him, would not abandon him, kissed him so that he would die feeling loved. And a spear point shattered Ben's clavicle; iron blade and bone chips shoved downward into his lungs. The sharp heave upon his pulmonary blood vessel shocked the fluid suddenly upstream, and it popped his heart. He died in an instant, Ari still drowning beside him.

On that rocky knoll that had been Saul's command post, just minutes before, he had had an army to command, but now the King saw his servants perish. These few had remained while scores of others had fled. Wise scores. Arrows, leaping up from the plane beyond the knoll's foot like happy dogs released to hunt, had bit his sons Malchishua and Abinadab, who would not now live out any stories worth preserving. They bit even Jonathan, his complicated hope. Jonathan, I built it all for you, what you would have given away to your friend. Oh, Jonathan, the pain of this arrow through my arm is less than the pain of my grief.

The Philistines have not yet climbed the rise. They will take me and humiliate me, leash me through the streets like a wild dog caught, zoo me for the amusement of the citizens of Ashkelon. Or else some shmuck will ever after get to brag he killed me. Still more vividly than spittle and chains, he imagined the flaming weight of his own heart, dropping through his bowels, flaring away his vitals, landing upon his testicles with an enduring sickliness, and then burning away all that might remain of the puny stuff of his kingship. Little ants of humiliation busied around inside his brain, carrying, exchanging, and setting down their little sand grits of hatred. Each facet of each grain revealed the face of another Israelite he'd let down, and he saw each sifting face's intolerable eyes.

This life hasn't worked. Cut my losses. "Boy!" His armor bearer, retreat cut off, had stayed. "Draw your sword. Cut me through the heart." Lifting his tunic to expose his chest, "Now!"

My master's ultimate perversion, to cast his armor bearer's soul into iniquity. His own final sin to damn me, too. "No."

This moment called for decisive action. He drew his own sword—frightening the armor bearer, who then drew his blade in order to parry—and plunged the hilt into the ground. The sword stood point up. He stripped off his tunic, and from his full regal height (the tallest man in Israel), he tipped rigidly forward.

That's one ending. (It goes on. The little armor bearer, like a secondary character in some Greek tragedy, overcome by all that he has seen, fell on his own sword—with, as it turns out, more accuracy than had his master. Then there's the Philistine occupation of a divided and demoralized Israel, the symbolic mutilation and display of the royal corpses, and the loyal Jabeshites' rescuing of their decapitated liberator to give him a dignified cremation. But that's not Saul's story. He's gone.) Here's another ending:

Dumbshit couldn't even fall down right: stabbed himself through the meaty part of the shoulder, missing vital organs and major blood vessels. It bit like a son of a bitch, but worst of all, he could still feel the fear. The pain was nothing compared to the awful consciousness of still being.

He heard and looked up at, not a Philistine gloater nor one of his own surviving troops, but—he didn't know how—some civilian stranger. "Who are you?"

Clear distaste in his swarthy eyes. No pity, only the disdain Saul felt he deserved.

He (who would later go brag to David, expecting reward, receiving instead a knife in the belly) said, "An Amalekite."

"I thought I killed all you guys."

The face did not change. The hatred did not perceptibly deepen. "Missed one."

And then the Amalekite said, "Surely the bitterness of death is past."

The bastard dares to quote him, the man I have come to revere. "Finish me off. Please."

The sweet appeasement of my vengeful anger. For my mother, my sisters I saw raped and stabbed while I hid cowardly who should have died defending them, I shall recover my honor.

But to dispatch him would mean to diminish, to call to an end the suffering he deserves. I see the quiver of his muscles and the more than physical torment in his eyes. He asks me to rescue him from Hell.

And so paused the Hamlet of the Amalekites. But alone with Hitler, would you hesitate?

"Please?"

"Your servant." Hack. Saul's head rolled. The executioner took the royal diadem and armband for his evidence.

And though I hate to do it, I must give David the final word. (Yes, it cleared his way to kingship, and yes, the Amalekite, as a bonus, let him publicize what happens to regicides, and yes, the old man had several times tried to kill him. He had many reasons to be glad that Saul was gone, but still. Sure, it's easy to get sentimental about an old enemy who is no longer a threat, and Jonathan was as much a richly useful political connection as a friend, but still. God damn him, the guy was a literary genius, and both these men, Jonathan and Saul, had loved him, and he must have felt something in return.) He composed a song for Jonathan and Saul:

Israel's beauty on the heights lies slain.
     Oh, how the mighty have fallen!
Tell it not in Gath, shout it
     not in the streets of Ashkelon,
     lest the daughters of the Philistines
     delight, lest the daughters
     of the uncircumcised cry
     their brothers' triumph.
Let there fall no dew from Gilboa's hills.
     Let there fall no rain
     upon your fields, no blessings
     on your altars, Gilboa, for the shield
     of the mighty is cast in the mud, the shield
     of Saul, unpolished, rusts.
From the blood of the slain, from the warrior's belly,
     Jonathan's bow draws back
     to spring, Saul's blade never
     turned back dry.
Saul and Jonathan, lovely and loved
     in their life, and in death, paired. They were swifter
     than eagles and stronger
     than lions.
O daughters of Israel, cry over Saul,
     who clad you in crimson and decked you in gold.
How the mighty have fallen.
     Jonathan! Slain upon the peak of your—
O Jonathan, my brother, I miss you!
     You were dear to me. Your love
     more wonderful, beyond the love of any woman.
How the mighty have fallen,
     and the weapons of war are lost.

Amos
Amos 1-9

He stood before the market square throng and bellowed out his prophecy. His mind blazed of God and right. His words burned. Simple as that.

Of course not.

He knew he'd have only a day, probably less, two tops, before he got, at best, the bum's rush back to the hills, at worst (and more likely), his head upon a warning spike before the palace. This was not a time of reasoned political debate over the issues of the day. Power spoke. Shepherds did not. Shepherds starved patiently, and the owners of the flocks ate lamb.

And that's what had gotten to him.

The Greeks would learn, in a couple or so more centuries, that bored shepherds—as they fought bugs, wolves, winters, and starvation—could invent lyric poetry. Offer them an annual contest, and you can coax them away from their flocks (to which they knew they might return to find them stolen, scattered irretrievably, or consumed by predators—but by God they'd risk it all for the petty glamour of literary fame) and into town to chant. City boys who'd never tasted Rocky Mountain oyster would bleach all the pain out, call it pastoral verse, and write their soft-core erotic fantasies into meadowy settings. Real shepherds, in the first quickening kick of classical Greek culture, would mutter out their drafts in total isolation—no fair Phyllis within sight to whom they could address their plaints unless they named their flocks. A whole year alone to refine and memorize— nothing else to do but their jobs. What, ultimately, is a pastoral love poem, but a plea for companionship? The townsfolk who would judge them would see in their eyes the fire of poetic inspiration. That wasn't fire; it was hunger, loneliness, and desperation. For a moment, as long as lasts my song, I am not an outcast slave. My whole life, I'm pouring into this verse; nothing else matters, certainly not the rest of my impoverished life. When the people at the center start to imitate and polish the cultural productions of the margins, then, for better or worse, you've got yourselves a civilization.

Power of bored shepherds. The ancient Jews had their David legend: shepherd boy comes down from the hills and deathwhacks a Goliath. It had been there all the time, but Amos was the first to figure out how to use it. Same miserable life, but a different tradition.

Two years before the big earthquake, when Uzziah was King of Judah and Jeroboam the son of Joash was King of Israel, Amos, a herdsman from Tekoa, a little place in Judah, came down to the market square in Bethel, on the edge of the Kingdom of Israel, and gave a speech. This guy nobody had ever seen before stood up on a stone and began to shout.

"The Lord," he said,

> will roar from Zion,

and his voice

> will resound from Jerusalem.

Even the shepherds shall hear it,

> and they shall mourn.

Even the top of Mount Carmel shall hear it

> and shall whither at the sound.

Thus saith the Lord:

> for three transgressions of Damascus, and for four,
> > I will not turn away the punishment thereof
> > because they have threshed Gilead with
> > > threshing instruments of iron.
> But I will send a fire into the house of Hazael which
> > shall devour the palaces of Benhadad.
> I will break the bolt on the gate of Damascus
> > and cut off the inhabitants from the plain of Aven
> > and him that holds the scepter from the house of Eden,
> And the people of Syria shall go into captivity,
> > exiled into Kir,
> > > saith the Lord.

Thus saith the Lord:

> for three transgressions of Gaza, and for four,
> > I will not turn away the punishment thereof[1]
> > because they carried away
> > > captives and enslaved them into Edom.

---

[1]You can see he's catching a rhythm and a pattern here that he'd long been practicing upon his sheep. Once he's found his groove, he can keep this up all day.

But I will send a fire onto the wall of Gaza which
        shall devour the palaces within.
I will cut off Gaza from Ashdod
        and him who holds the scepter from Ashkelon,
        and I will turn my hand against Ekron.
And the remnant of the Philistines
        shall perish,
                saith the Lord.

Thus saith the Lord:
    for three transgressions of Tyre, and for four,
            I will not turn away the punishment thereof[2]
        because they carried away
                slaves into Edom
            and remembered not our covenant of brotherhood.
    But I will send a fire
            to the walls of Tyre
                which shall devour the Phoenician palaces.

Thus saith the Lord:
    for three transgressions of Edom, and for four,
            I will not turn away the punishment thereof
        because he pursued his brother with the sword
                and cast off all pity
                and his anger did tear perpetually
                and he kept his wrath forever.
    But I will send a fire upon Teman which
            shall devour the palaces of Bozrah.

---

[2]At this point, however, you might start to recognize the pattern. I'm going to write it out because I've committed myself, but in this foreign policy part of the speech, he's saying pretty much the same thing about the Syrians, the Philistines, the Phoenicians, the Edomites, the Ammonites, and the Moabites. Sure, he's setting down a rhythm, but he's also just walked into the square, and he's collecting his audience. He's vamping: gathering the crowd and focusing their attention before he starts in on what he really wants them to hear. Feel free to skip the next four strophes and come back when he starts in on Judah.

Thus saith the Lord:

    for three transgressions of the children of Ammon, and for four,

        I will not turn away the punishment thereof

        because they have

            ripped up the women with child in Gilead

            just to enlarge their border.

But I will kindle a fire in the wall of Rabbah

        and it shall devour the palaces

            with shouting in the day of battle,

            with a tempest in the day of the whirlwind.

And their king shall go into captivity

        he and his princes together,

            saith the Lord.

Thus saith the Lord:

    for three transgressions of Moab, and for four

        I will not turn away the punishment thereof

        because he burned the bones of the King

        of Edom into lime.

But I will send a fire upon Moab,

        and it shall devour the palaces of Kerioth,

            and Moab shall die with tumult, with

            shouting, and with the sound of the trumpet.

And I will cut off their judge from their midst,

        and I will slay all the princes with him,

            saith the Lord.

Thus saith the Lord:

    for three transgressions of Judah, and for four

        I will not turn away the punishment thereof[3]

---

[3] OK, come on back now. Notice now when he gets to the Jewish kingdoms of Judah and Israel, he treats them no differently from the Gentile nations. They're just as bad. He's in Israel, but he's starting off with Judah, just another foreign power. But that's where he's from, so is Judah his real target, much safer to aim at from rival Israel than at home? When he gets to Israel next, he's, perhaps, just coming off as even handed. But it is also the point when he offers his neck to the blade.

because they have despised the law of the Lord and
> have not kept his commandments, and
> their own lies led them into error
>> in which their fathers had walked as well.
But I will send fire upon Judah,
> and it shall devour the palaces of Jerusalem.

Mad as he was, he must have known now that he was about to enter dangerous territory. In ancient kingdoms, there was no free speech, and he was not among the guild of prophets, the mad holy men who lived on alms and the divine breath, honored by all for speaking ceaselessly an absolute spiritual truth that was never recorded and that no one remembers. But Nathan, a different kind of prophet, one who had grounded upon the Earth the divine word's burning charge, had challenged King David for his sinfulness. There, Amos must have thought, is my warrant. There is my precedent. I've gathered a crowd, and this is what I came for.

Thus saith the Lord:
> for three transgressions of Israel, and for four
>> I will not turn away the punishment thereof
>> because they sold the righteous for silver
>>> and the poor for a pair of shoes.
They pant after the dust of the earth,
>> lock the poor from it, turn them from the gate,
>> and take it for themselves.
A man and his father go in unto the same maid
> and thus profane My Holy Name.
They lay themselves down upon
>> clothes pledged to the altar, and
>> they drink in the house of their gods
>>> wine collected as a fine
>>>> upon the wicked.

Yet I destroyed the Amorites before you, men
> tall as the cedars,
> strong as the oaks;
I destroyed
> their fruit from above,
> their roots from below.

And I led you up
  from the land of Egypt,
and I led you up
  for forty years through the Wilderness
  to possess the land of the Amorites.
I raised up your sons to be prophets and your young men
  to be Nazarites:
      Is that not so? Is that not so, O children of Israel?
        saith the Lord.
But you got the Nazarites drunk,
  and you commanded the prophets
    that they prophecy no more.

Behold, I will therefore press down upon you as
  a load of sheaves presses down upon a cart
    so that the swift
      shall lose their speed
    and the strong
      their force,
    nor shall the mighty
      save himself.
    Nor shall the bowman stand,
    nor the swift of foot,
    nor the horseman.
And the stout-hearted among the mighty shall, that day,
    flee naked,
      saith the Lord.

Hear this word that the Lord hath spoken against
  you, O children of Israel, against
  the whole family which I brought
    up from the land of Egypt, saying,
  You only have I known of all the families of the Earth,
    and therefore,
  I will punish you
    for all your sins.

Can two walk together except they be agreed?
Will a lion roar in the forest when he has no prey?
Will a young lion cry out from his den unless he has no food?
Can a bird fall into a trap where there is no snare?
Will a hunter retrieve a net that has taken nothing?
Will a trumpet blow in the city and the people feel no fear?
Shall there be evil in the city and the Lord do nothing?
 Yes, the Lord will do nothing
   unless he reveals
     his secret to his servants, the prophets.
The lion has roared. Who will not fear?
The Lord hath spoken. Who will not prophesy?

Tell them in the palaces of Ashdod
 and in the palaces of Egypt
to come assemble themselves on the mountains in Samaria
 to see the confusion among the people there
 and the oppression of the people there.
How's that going to look to the rest of the world?
For they do not know how to do right,
   saith the Lord,
 who store up violence and robbery in their palaces.

Therefore, thus saith the Lord God:
 An adversary shall there be all round the land
   who will bring down your strength
   and spoil your palaces.
Thus saith the Lord:
 as a shepherd saves from the mouth of a lion
   two legs,
   a piece of an ear,
 so shall the children of Israel who dwell in Samaria be saved:
   in Damascus, they'll give you
     the corner of a bed, maybe a couch—
    all they'd reserve
     for a concubine slave.
Hear ye, and testify in the House of Jacob!

saith the Lord God, the God of hosts,
On the day I visit the transgressions of Israel upon them, I will also
visit the altars of Bethel, and the horns of the altar
shall be cut off and let fall to the ground.
I will smite the winter house with the summer house,
the houses of ivory shall perish,
and the great houses shall end,
saith the Lord.

Hear this, you cows (that's what you are) of Bashan,
lazily grazing away upon the mountainsides of Samaria,
munching away at what the poor produce for you,
stepping upon and crushing the needy—imagine
the laziness of a cow who calls
out to his betters, "Here, boy, bring me
something to drink."
The Lord God has sworn, has sworn upon—

Going by the translations available to me, I imagine Amos pausing here. Yes, he'd worked on this speech for months, and he'd thought he was ready. But it wasn't so much memorized as outlined. This was, after all, an oral culture, and the spoken word was a set of riffs upon which the prophet would play, chords available to fill out the overall structure. Verbal surprises could still arise as he happened to hit those chords in novel ways. To swear upon something: an oft-hit note on the oral poet's keyboard. For the Lord to swear—OK. "Upon"—edging toward dissonance now, for what can out-holy the Lord Himself? What does a good jazz musician do who has followed a solo's logic into a blind corner? Plunge straight into that dissonant sound, embrace it, and make it swing.

upon His own holiness,
that the days are coming when the Lord Himself
will snag you with fishhooks and
leave your posterity flopping in the bottom of the boat.
And (to get back to that cow metaphor once again)
I'll crack the walls in your palaces so that
I can shove every one of you cows out through
the breaches.

Come to Bethel and rebel, go to Gilgal and rebel some more,
    and then make your tithe offering, why don't you.
Go on, saith the Lord,
    and offer your thanksgiving bread, your freewill offerings, for
        you love making a big show of that, don't you?
            Thus saith the Lord.

You know what I'll give you
    out of the abundance of my love for you?
    Clean teeth.
That's right, perfect dental health
    because you'll get no bread. I'll
        make you starve. Look,
            I've been doing it already,
    and still you won't return to me,
        saith the Lord.

And also,
    saith the Lord,
look what else I've done to you,
    and it's like you haven't even noticed
        it is I who
        have done it:
hold back the rains.
    Three months to go before harvest, when most
        you needed it.
    One place no rain, another plenty;
        one place has thrived and
        another place withered.
So two or three dry cities migrated into one wet,
    where there
        was not enough for all.
Yet still you have not returned to me,
    saith the Lord.

I hit your crops with diseases: blast and mildew.
When your gardens, vineyards, figs, and olives had

just started to fruit,
    I sent the locusts to devour them.
Yet still you have not returned to me,
    saith the Lord.

I've sent you the Egyptian plague,
I've slain your men with the sword,
I've stolen your horses,
I've made a great stink in your armed camps
    (and I'm not talking metaphorically here—you
    know the reek I'm talking about),
Yet still you have not returned to me,
    saith the Lord.

I have done unto you as I did
    to Sodom and Gomorrah. And the rest of you, who live,
    are but a brand I've plucked from that burning.
Yet still you have not returned to me,
    saith the Lord.

It's like nothing I've done yet can reach you guys.
    Therefore,
    Israel—I mean Israel specifically—
I will do this
    to you, and because I will do this, you must
    prepare to meet your God.
    O Israel!
For lo, He that forms the mountains,
    and creates the wind,
    and declares unto men his thought,
    who makes both the darkness and the dawn,
    who walks in the high places of the Earth,
The Lord, the God of Hosts, is His Name!

And at this point, Amos stopped a moment. His throat was dry, and his voice was straining with that searing list of punishments that didn't work. He was building up toward describing a major curse, and he had his audience hooked and dangling. But he couldn't pause too long. If they thought too deeply, they'd arrest him. Got to keep them drawn in by the flow of words. Two large gulps from his leather flask, and back to work.

The patter's a distraction. So long as soldiers and royal functionaries are listening, they aren't acting. Their action would be, of course, to arrest him. As the con man's patter moves the mark along, keeping him from thinking through the situation, here too, the prophet turns their attention toward a socially acceptable "Come to the Lord" and keeps the political end of that rope concealed in his hand.

Two more large gulps from his leather flask, then back to work.

No. He looked at the crowd again and saw the fear sinking in: the sunken eyes, the slack mouths, the tension in the shoulders. The curse is accomplished, and they believe me. These people don't need another thunderbolt; they need comfort. As a starving mother with an empty breast cannot feed a hungry child, still she can hold and caress her baby to show the abundance of her impotent love. My message now shall be, I'm with you. In this rock land where all of us may perish, yes, I'm with you.

Hear, O Israel, the word I take up next will be
    a lamentation for you.
The virgin of Israel is fallen,
    and she shall no more rise. She lies
    spread out on the ground. There is none to raise her up.

For thus saith the Lord God:
    the city that went forth by a thousand
        shall have but a hundred left,
    and the city that went forth by a hundred
        shall have remaining but ten—all
    that shall be left of the house of Israel.

For thus saith the Lord unto the house of Israel:
    Seek me, and live.

Not in Bethel, nor Gilgal, nor Beersheba,
    for Gilgal shall go into captivity,
    and Bethel shall come to nothing—
        those are just places.
Seek instead, the Lord Himself,

not places of His worship,
    lest He break out like fire in the house of Joseph,
        and there be none to quench it in Bethel.

You who turn justice into wormwood and leave
    righteousness lying on the ground,
seek Him
    who made the Pleides and Orion
        and turns the shadow of death into morning
        and makes the day dark with night,
    who calls for the waters of the sea
        and pours them out upon the face of the earth.
The Lord is His name,
    who strengthens the robbed against the strong
        so that those victims shall rise against the fortress.
In that fortress of the strong,
    they hate him that rebukes them at the gate,
    and they despise him that speaks uprightly.

That's me.

At this point now, he ceased his speaking to the crowd, and he speaks instead for it—his voice still forward, but body and gestures now turned toward the great houses, too subtly, he hoped, for meathead soldiers to notice, too natural for anyone to hold it against him as intentional. Yes, come all you to the Lord, but it's to the big-time sinners now that I speak.

Therefore,
    because you have trodden on the poor,
        and you take from them burdens of wheat,
        listen to what shall become of you:
you have built houses of hewn stone,
        but you shall not live in them;
you have planted precious vineyards,
        but you shall not drink their wine.
For I know your manifold transgressions and your mighty sins:
    you oppress the just,
    you take bribes,
    you turn away the needy at the gate.

[Full face upon the crowd now, starting off quietly, then building:]

Therefore,
>   the prudent (unlike me) shall keep silent,
>   for it is an evil time.

So here's my advice to you:
>   Seek good and not evil so that you may live and
>>   so the Lord, God of Hosts shall be with you.
>   Hate evil, and love goodness; do justice by
>>   the beggars at your gate.
>   It may thus be that the Lord God of Hosts will deal graciously
>>   with the remnant of Joseph.

Therefore,
>   the Lord God of Hosts, the Lord saith thus:
>>   In all the city streets, lamentations,
>>   and they shall cry on all the highways, "Alas! Alas!"
>>   and those who have learned lamentation
>>>   shall meet the plowman in the field
>>>   and teach him, too, to mourn.
>>   After I've passed through the vineyards,
>>>   you shall hear a keening there,
>>>>   saith the Lord.

Woe unto those who have wished for their Lord's coming!
Why would you wish for the day of the Lord—for deliverance?
>   The day of the Lord, I tell you, is darkness, not light.
It's as if a man fled from a lion and he met a bear,
>   as if he ran home, leaned his hand against a wall,
>>   and a snake bit him.
Won't the day of the Lord be darkness, not light—
>   very dark, no brightness at all?

I hate, I despise your feast days,
>   and I will not smell the smoke from your solemn assemblies.

Though you send me burnt offerings of meat,
  I will not accept them.
Neither will I regard the peace offerings of your fat beasts.
Take away from me the noise of your songs. The music of your harps,
  I will not hear.

I'll tell you what I want instead.
This. Hear me now. This is the primary message:
  Let justice roll down like waters
  and righteousness like a mighty stream.

Did you send me sacrifices and meal-offerings
  in the desert for forty years, O Israel?
But you have borne the tabernacles of Moloch
  the images of Chiun,
  the star of Kochav,
  the gods you made yourselves.
Therefore,
  I will exile you beyond Damascus
      saith the Lord,
      whose name is the God of Hosts.

The strong oppress the weak, and God sides with the weak. He sides with the just and the merciful, the generous and the broken-hearted, not the pious. We all face exile and death. The suffering have little to fear in death, the destitute little to lose, and the homeless as little shelter in exile as in the land of their fathers. The lowly, I cannot threaten; they've been given little that can be taken. They survive on mouthfuls of hope. The prosperous can lose their prosperity in so many ways, exile and death just two. Them, I can threaten with the loss of actual bread—richly flavorful and delicately crafted at that, a revelation of texture and scent. They have been lent much, and the debt is due.

Let justice roll down like waters and righteousness like a mighty stream.

How do I make them heed?

That last bit, by the way, that God wants justice, not sacrifice, inaugurates the classical era of ancient Israelite prophecy. (Or perhaps it doesn't, and that message was written back into it later in the classical era—I'll get to that point later.) Isaiah, Hosea, and Micah would later take it up and insist upon it. Prophecy, from now on, is no longer ineffable, but practical.

Woe to those
　　who repose at ease in Zion
and to those
　　who trust in the mountain of Samaria,
in both Judah and Israel, those
　　who call yourselves chiefs of the nations.
The whole house of Israel has come. They're at your door.

Go to Calneh and see; from there
go to Hamath the great, then
go down into Gath of the Philistines.
　　Are they better than these kingdoms of yours?
　　Are their borders more broad than your own?

You bring yourselves nearer to the evil day
　　and draw ever closer to the seat of violence,
　　who lie upon beds of ivory,
　　who eat lambs from the flock and calves from the stalls,
　　who sing to the harp (and think, in your conceit,
　　　　　you sound like David),
　　who drink wine by the bowlful
　　and spritz yourselves with the finest perfumes.

Therefore,
　　they'll be led away now at the head of the line of exiles,
　　and that banquet that was set before them shall be taken away.
The Lord God of Hosts hath sworn by—

[Again, that moment when control is lost]

　　—by Himself.
Thus saith the Lord God of Hosts:
　　I abhor the pride of Jacob,
　　and I hate his palaces;
Therefore,
　　I will hand over the city

and all things therein.
I will destroy you so thoroughly that if
I see ten men left
in one last house, even they
shall die.

The kinsman shall come to recover the dead,[4]
to recover the bones left burnt in the burnt house,
and he'll call inside, "Anybody in there?"
And someone will answer, "No."
And the kinsman will say, "Shut up!"
He'll listen again,
    pretend the silence this time is his answer,
    then give the order to take out the bones
and not mention the name of the Lord.

The Lord commands. At his orders,
    the great houses shall be cloven to splinters
    and the small houses ground into chips.

Would you run your horses over rocks
or plow those rocks with your oxen?
    I think you might,
for you have shown bad judgment,
    having perverted

----

[4]In this next strophe, I'm trying to represent one of those verses in the Bible that has been so mangled in the transmission that it doesn't make much sense. Maybe some copyist got a little bit of the verse wrong, and then another copyist, working from that copy, just repeated the errors, and as later copyists tried to make some sense out of it, they introduced more errors, and whatever the line was at first, it's now irretrievably lost. Look, since I don't know Hebrew, in working up this piece I've read a few different translations of Amos, and for this verse every one of them is different. When they each try to make sense out the original in a different way, that tells me the original is a mess. And however they translate it, it barely fits the context—since the rest of the book seems more fluently organized, that too tells me there's something wrong with this verse. Anyway, here's my attempt.

Shibboleth

sweet justice into gall and
the fruit of righteousness into hemlock.
You've rejoiced in something worth nothing. It's like
you've congratulated yourselves on growing horns,
to which I'd say, "Really? Show me the point."

But look,
I will raise up a nation against you, O house of Israel,
saith the Lord God of Hosts,
and they shall bulldoze over you all the way
from the approaches to Hamath to the brook of Arabah.

Here is what the Lord God showed me:
out in the hayfield, He formed grasshoppers
just as the first shoots of the second growth were rising,
the one the farmers would get to keep
after the first and sweetest mowing
went to the king.
When those grasshoppers had consumed all the forage,
then I said,
O Lord God, forgive us!
Please, I beseech you. I get
the symbolism, really.
Jacob is now so small, how shall he rise again?
And the Lord relented.
It shall not be,
saith the Lord.

Here is what the Lord God showed me:
He called forth fire,
and it consumed the great deep,
and it consumed the field, too.
Then I said,
O Lord God, cease!
Please, I beseech you.
Jacob is now so small, how shall he rise again?
And the Lord relented.

It shall not be,
saith the Lord.

Here is what the Lord God showed me:
The Lord Himself stood upon a wall
built with a plumbline,
and He held a plumbline.
And the Lord said to me, "Amos,
what do you see?"
And I said to Him, "Well,
I see a plumbline."
And the Lord said, "Behold,
I will set a plumbline in the midst of my people, Israel.
Don't expect me back;
don't expect me to forgive a stone
out of line.
The high places of Isaac shall be desolate,
the sanctuaries of Israel shall be ruined,
and I will rise
against the house of Jeroboam with the sword."

Amaziah, the priest of Bethel, had been listening. The threats up till just this point had been vague, general, and symbolic—nothing outright treasonous. That last line, however, was going too far, naming and threatening Jeroboam, the King of Israel, personally.

In the ancient world, no one expected the lower classes to be happy. You were either rich or poor, and nobody wanted to be poor, but most people were, they didn't like it, and that's the way life worked. The poor had exactly enough to survive on—maybe a little less, not a barley-grain more—and the rich skimmed off any margin above the barest survival.

Amos was calling this unfair. Well, yeah, everybody knew that. His innovation, however, was to call this a perversion of God's will rather than an inscrutable expression of it. You are not a starveling because that is the place the Lord has, in His wisdom, assigned you. No, you starve because the wealthy feast. The skim is not the nature of things, but a sin.

While, from a professional viewpoint, Amaziah found this novel moral theology intriguing, he knew also that his own social standing and his personal wellbeing depended more upon the good will of the skimmers than of the skimmed. So he sent word to the King: "This guy Amos has entered the country, and he openly conspires against you. He's such a talker, the land can't bear all his words. Here's part of what he said: 'Jeroboam shall die by the sword, and Israel shall be led into exile.'"

But he couldn't wait for a royal response by return messenger. Amos continued to speak, and people were taking it in. He had to act. His first priestly option was a rebuke. Religious authority usually cows them.

"Amos! You call yourself a seer. Ha! Run on home to Judah. Don't think I can't see what's going on here. They're paying you for this subversive 'prophecy,' aren't they? Well, go back and prophesy where you're earning your bread for it. But not here. This is totally inappropriate—right in the town where the King himself holds court."

Amos started off with a chuckle. "Look, I'm no prophet, I'm not the son of a prophet, and so, no, I don't have the guild-training of the professionals. I'm a herdsman. And as for the bread, out in the hills, I live mostly on wild figs. Nobody from Judah sent me. The Lord grabbed me by the whiskers and tipped my head back to look at Him while I should have been following my flock, and He said, 'Go prophesy to my people Israel.' So here I am."

Amaziah: "You expect me to believe that?"

"Suit yourself."

Now, therefore, hear the word of the Lord:
> You say,
>> Prophesy not against Israel and
>> prophesy not against the house of Isaac.
> But the Lord saith,
>> Your wife shall take up prostitution,
>> your children shall be slain by the sword,
>> your land will be taken, divided, and distributed by lot,
>>> effacing all posterity,
>> and you shall die in a polluted land.
> Israel shall surely go into captivity.

At this point, at this moment of Amos's straight-up defiance of authority, I want to ask, how have these words come down to us? Since ancient monarchies did not recognize any freedom of speech, how did Amos's words, not to mention Amos himself, survive?

One possibility, maybe even the most likely, is that they didn't. This crazy shepherd starts spouting off in the marketplace, and the King's soldiers come in right away to cart him off, and nobody ever hears any news of him again. The unrecorded end of his story involved either a quick sword thrust or a slow starvation in chains.

However, that somebody would have the guts to speak up like that stuck in the popular memory. An oral tradition developed around him. Admirers placed in his mouth words they would have liked to hear. He became an oratorical Robin Hood. A tradition gelled around a general outline, a set of repeated formulas, and a pattern of anaphora for a performer to improvise upon. Amos, like Homer, became the name, not of a poet, but of a bardic tradition that circulated orally a long time before it was ever written down. But unlike the aristocratic Homeric tradition, Amos would be a peasant tradition. Peasants would sing or hear the tune and know that God was on their side.

Its first setting down in ink, in this case, was probably in Judah. If it was before Assyria destroyed the Kingdom of Israel, then the scribes of the rival Kingdom of Judah who set down a polished version of the tradition may have seen it as useful anti-Israel propaganda. On the other hand, it may have, like a lot of other traditions, come to Judah along with refugees after the fall of Israel and have been written down only then. Either way, it could become a usefully oblique criticism of the Judahite monarchy under the guise of a historical document of unrest in Israel. And it was a precedent and a warrant for the preachings of the other prophets who followed him. Jeremiah and Isaiah took him as their model for speaking in the name of the Lord.

It could be also that Amos actually composed, rehearsed, and spoke these words before the market crowd at Bethel and a scribe took them down as he spoke them for use at his trial. Or it could be that Amos, having composed his speech in the hills, sought out a scribe to take it down, to make it permanent right from the start before he stood up to defy the authorities out loud. They may have cut him down before he ever finished, but it survived on paper, much copied (and much refined in the copying, with additional notes from later classical prophecy tucked into it; the final strophe, in fact, looks like a post-exilic addition) and much admired among the subversive intellectuals who could read it.

Least likely of all, we have his own words as he spoke them in the square, undistorted in transmission, taken down via some magical sort of transcription that was attentive from the first hail and that relied on no fallible human hands and ears. I can't imagine how that would have worked.

Forgive me this digression. Martin Luther King, Jr., thought the Book of Amos—for the grandeur and compassion of its moral vision, for the beauty of its poetry—was one of the most stirring passages in the Bible, and so do I. So I've been trying to see Amos rehearsing these words among his sheep, gripping a market day crowd with his stare, shouting down the priesthood. What could he have sounded like? What could this mad shepherd have been thinking? All I have to go on are the words, which I mangle in trying to imagine how this miracle of courage and eloquence could have happened. No story I weave out of it can stand up to the moral vision of his prophecy.

Here is what the Lord God showed me: Behold!
> A basket of summer fruit.

And he said,
> Amos, what do you see?

And I said (maybe being a bit too obvious here again, I thought),
> A basket of summer fruit.

Then the Lord said to me,
> The end is come for my people Israel.
> I will no longer pardon them.
> I will no longer pass among them.
> In that day, the songs in the temple shall be wailings,
>> saith the Lord God,
> everywhere corpses cast out,
> everywhere silence.

Hear this,
> you that swallow up the needy,
> you that cut off the poor from the land,
> you that say,
>> When will the new moon be gone
>>> that we may sell grain,
>> when will the Sabbath be done
>>> that we may open our stores of grain
>>> to sell them,
>>>> making the weight small
>>>> and the prices large,
>>>> perverting the scales,
>>> that we may buy the poor for silver
>>>> and the needy for a pair of shoes
>>>> and sell them the spoiled wheat?

The Lord has sworn by the excellence of Jacob,
> Surely, I will never forget their works.

Shall not the land quake for this
>> and everyone mourn that dwells therein?
>> The land shall rise up like a flood, and it will tremble,
>>> it will shake, it will
>>> cast off those who dwell therein who have not heeded,
>>> like those who
>>>> do not heed the rising floods of Egypt.

And it shall come to pass on that day,
>> saith the Lord God,
that I will cause the sun to go down at noon,
>> and I will darken the earth on a clear day.
I will turn your feasts into mourning
>> and all your songs into lamentations.
I will bring up rough sack cloth onto all loins
>> and baldness upon every head.
I will make it like the mourning over an only son.
It shall be a bitter day.

Behold, the days come,
>> saith the Lord God,
that I will send a famine into the land,
>> not a famine of bread
>> nor a thirst for water,
>>> but of hearing the word of the Lord.
And they shall wander from sea to sea and from the North to the East—
>> they shall run to and fro to seek the word of the Lord,
>> and they shall not find it.
In that day, the fair virgins and the young men
>> shall faint from thirst.
They that swear by the sin of Samaria and say,
>> O tribe of Dan, your God lives yet! or
>> The road to Beersheba remains yet free!—
>>> even they shall fall, never to rise again.

I saw the Lord standing beside an altar,

and He said,
Strike the lintel, and the doorposts shake.
Cut off the head, and the remnant members,
    I shall easily slay by the sword.
        Those who flee shall not get away;
        those who escape shall not be saved.
Though they dig down to hell,
    there My hand shall reach them;
though they climb to heaven,
    from there, I shall bring them down;
though they hide themselves at the peak of Carmel,
    I will search them out and take them;
though they hide from my sight on the floor of the sea,
    I will command the serpent, and it will bite them.
and though they go into captivity under the eyes of their enemies,
        even there
    I will command the sword that slays them.
    I will set My eye upon them for evil
        and not for good.

And the Lord God of Hosts,
    Who touches the land and it shudders
        so that all therein shall mourn
        because it shall rise up like a river
        that drowns them all, like the floods in Egypt;
    Who has built His upper stories in heaven
        and founded His troops on earth;
    Who calls for the waters of the sea
        and pours them out upon the face of the earth:
The Lord is his name.

Are you not to Me
    more dear than the children of the Cushites,
    O children of Israel?
        saith the Lord.
Have I not brought
    you out of the land of Egypt,

the Philistines out of Caphtor,
and the Syrians out of Kir?

Behold:
    the eyes of the Lord are upon
        the sinful kingdom,
            and I will destroy it from the face of the earth,
            but I will not destroy completely
        the house of Jacob,
    saith the Lord.

For I will command,
    and I will scatter the house of Israel among all nations
    as though shaken from a sieve, yet not
    the least seed shall fall upon the earth.
The sinners of My people shall die by the sword, those
    who say, "Evil cannot overtake us."

In that day, I will raise up the fallen tabernacle of David
    repair its cracks,
    restore its ruins, and
    rebuild it as in the old days
so that they may inherit
    the remnant of Edom
    and all the nations that call My name,
        saith the Lord who does all this.

Behold:
    the day comes,
        saith the Lord,
    when the plowman shall meet the reaper
    and the treader of grapes him that sows the seed,
    and the mountains shall drip sweet wine,
    and all the hills shall melt,
    and I will return from captivity
        my people Israel,
    and they shall build the wasted cities and inhabit them,

and they shall plant vineyards and drink the wine thereof,
and they shall plant gardens and eat the fruit.

I will plant them on their land,
and they shall no more be uprooted from their land
that I have given them,
saith the Lord your God.

And then, having said his piece, he went home. Or else, mad with loneliness and anger, he was silenced when he'd barely begun.

Made in the USA
Lexington, KY
15 January 2016